NIGHT SHADES

HARLOW DAIGER
AND
MARLEY DEL WOOD

FriesenPress

Suite 300 - 990 Fort St
Victoria, BC, V8V 3K2
Canada

www.friesenpress.com

Copyright © 2021 by Harlow Daiger and Marley Del Wood
First Edition — 2021

Edited by Melva McLean

All rights reserved.

No part of this publication may be reproduced in any form, or by any means, electronic or mechanical, including photocopying, recording, or any information browsing, storage, or retrieval system, without permission in writing from FriesenPress.

ISBN
978-1-03-910157-9 (Hardcover)
978-1-03-910156-2 (Paperback)
978-1-03-910158-6 (eBook)

1. FICTION, HORROR

Distributed to the trade by The Ingram Book Company

NIGHT SHADES

TABLE OF CONTENTS

1   **DEAR SISTER**
by H. Daiger

29   **THE INCIDENT IN MILLS**
by Marley Del Wood

51   **THE BOY IN THE HOLE**
by H. Daiger

85   **THE RIVER**
by Marley Del Wood

97   **IT SHOULD HAVE BEEN ME**
by H. Daiger

115   **WILD CHILD**
by Marley Del Wood

DEAR SISTER

IT'S DARK OUT THERE TONIGHT, she thought, staring through the windshield. The glow from the dashboard lights gave her a ghostly reflection in the rear-view mirror, and the tires of the old jeep crunched noisily on the gravel road until it abruptly gave way to wild grass and dirt. She'd been driving for over two hours and, with the moon being only a sliver of light in the sky, the headlights were the only window into what lay ahead down the uneven road. She'd ventured down this lonely trail on September 4th every year for as long as she could remember, but this year was very different.

The cornfields on both sides of the road suddenly ended, and birch trees loomed into the circle of her headlights. An overgrown path, guarded by the towering sentinels with peeling bark, led to the old family plot. Branches scraped the sides of the SUV as their shadows stretched greedily ahead of her. She drove carefully until she reached the inner tree line. The tall grasses, deadened by a recent frost, swayed like a living thing in the beams of her headlights. The copse of surrounding trees ringed the graveyard, hiding its inhabitants from the rest of the world. She'd never minded the seclusion before, but tonight the meadow had taken on an otherworldly feel.

She slowed to a stop, slid the gear shift to park, and shut off the SUV. She sat for a moment, listening to the *tick, tick* of the engine cooling, then blew out a breath in a satisfied sigh. She reached over, removed a small flashlight from the glove compartment, grabbed a couple of bags from the floor of the passenger side, and stepped out into the night. It was still technically summer, but the chill in the air and heady scent of loam had set the stage for an early fall.

She quietly closed her door, not wanting to interrupt the stillness of the graveyard, and shivered as she started walking. She took careful steps, using the flashlight to avoid the occasional weathered headstone cloaked by nature until she crested a small hill near the far edge of the clearing. She stood there for a moment, listening to the distant hoot of an owl before making her way down an incline. She stopped at the base of an old dead tree with its centre having been split long ago by a lightning strike. She dropped her bags, spread out an old blanket and set out a bottle of red wine, a plastic glass and fork, and a piece of blueberry pie wrapped in cellophane.

She sat down with her back to the tree, poured and sipped her wine, listening to the breeze rustle through the leaves. She had been anxious about coming out alone for the first time. She took a long swig of wine to finish what was in her glass and poured another.

"You know?" she said to the surrounding night. "I'll admit I was a little nervous about coming out here. I wasn't sure what I would say, or even do. Old habits die hard, I guess."

Then she poured a bit of wine on the ground next to her as an offering. Small droplets of reddened mud splashed onto the sun-bleached jawbone of the half-buried human skeleton that lay at the base of the tree. Its skull rested peacefully on one curled arm, as if it had simply laid down for an afternoon nap.

***

This is the kind of stress that gives people ulcers, Lee thought as she carefully drove the speed limit down Faithful Avenue. She was in no hurry to get to Lucy's. Her mind was reeling with possible outcomes of the conversation she was about to have with her sister, and it was making her feel quite nauseated. For the most part, Lucy was usually aloof and uninterested in Lee's boyfriends…until they hung around for longer than Lucy felt was necessary. Then she simply acted like an asshole until they left. Her reasons were along the lines of "he was a loser," or "he wasn't good enough for you," and Lee's favourite: "I'm sure he was cheating, anyway…" Lee knew that her sister was being controlling and manipulative. However, she also knew Lucy was right: these men weren't necessarily good for her; they were usually reckless, immature, and irresponsible. It had occurred to Lee that perhaps she had chosen them because they were direct opposites of what she herself needed to be. They made her feel free of her perpetual burdens, even if the feeling was fleeting. Deep down, though, she knew they lacked staying power and never fought to keep them. Scott, her current boyfriend, was different.

Lee let out an audible sigh as she pulled into the parking lot and sat for a moment, taking in the sun's warmth.

Okay, she thought. *Do I ease her into it? Or blurt it out? Tell her we've been dating for a while? Or lie and tell her I just met him? Butter her up with tickets to a concert? Or...actually, fuck it! I don't need to buy my sister's approval.*

Lucy's reaction, Lee was certain, would be one of three variations. There was the open-mouthed scowl as if Lee had just slapped her across the face, the ridiculous sobbing that turned into a full-on ugly cry as if Lee had run over her puppy, and Lucy's favourite: the calm before the storm. This last reaction involved various phases. There was the silent treatment, followed by sometimes weeks of one-word answers, steely glances, and rigid gestures before the unpredictable—but not unexpected—explosive tornado. The severity, of course, was dependent on the level of betrayal Lucy felt.

Most sisters wouldn't put up with this, but then again, most sisters weren't identical twins. Lee had always felt like taking care of Lucy was the same as taking care of herself. On that thought, Lee grabbed her purse and went inside.

***

"Jesus, would you spill it already? I can feel you vibrating from here," Lucy said as she handed Lee a coffee. As usual they sat in the kitchen at the table—not the living room, because Lucy didn't like messing it up. Heaven forbid anyone lived in the living room. She only had a couple of mugs and always gave Lee the one sporting Marvin the Martian, with his perpetually perplexed look and "Where's the kaboom?" slogan.

Oh, it's coming, Marvin, Lee thought. She took a deep breath.

"I'm waiting," Lucy said, smiling in anticipation.

"You know what? I'm not sugar-coating this. I'm in love. His name is Scott Turner, and I've been dating him for almost a year. He's good for me, and he's not going anywhere. So you have to be okay with this."

Lee looked Lucy dead in the eyes and waited for a dramatic response. She wasn't disappointed.

"Lee-Anne…did you say almost a year? Are you serious?" Lucy's smile quickly faded. She gave Lee the most shockingly hurt face she could muster.

Lee set her coffee on the table, then leaned back with her arms folded.

"We both know why I kept this to myself. I'm pretty sure my last ex still has a restraining order on you," she said in jest to lighten the blow; it didn't work.

Lee could see that Lucy was genuinely upset. Lucy was sitting across from her on the edge of her chair, hands under her knees, and staring at the floor. Lee decided that guilting her sister for past behaviours wouldn't solve anything because she was right. Keeping something like this from your sister *was* shitty.

Lee softened her tone.

"Look, I didn't keep this a secret to punish you. I would love nothing more than to be able to share stuff like this, but you're always so jealous and annoyed when I get a boyfriend."

"I'm not jealous. I've only ever looked out for you," Lucy said, then sipped her coffee without making eye contact.

"This one is different. He's kind, smart, and incredibly funny. He's respectful, sweet, and he loves me. You will like him if you give him a fair chance," Lee pleaded.

Lee sipped her coffee and gave Lucy a moment to absorb her comments. She thought about how much she hated confrontation, while Lucy seemed to thrive on it at times, and wondered how twins could be so different.

"You said the other idiots were kind and funny, too," Lucy muttered.

"Just—please, for the love of all that is pure and holy, would it kill you to be nice?" Lee was getting frustrated. They were at the point where she thought Lucy was about to start crying or yelling at her for this "ultimate betrayal." She jumped a bit when Lucy suddenly shifted her weight in her chair to lean forward.

"Relax, Lee. I'm not mad. I didn't even notice you weren't coming around as much as you used to. How fucked up is that? I get it, I haven't always been so open-minded at the thought of sharing you with others, because you're all I have left. So fine, I'll try to give him a chance, but this doesn't mean I won't speak up if I think he's a douche."

"Um, o-okay," Lee stammered.

Despite what Lucy had just said, the conversation was going better than she'd anticipated. "Are you busy tomorrow? I thought you could come to my place after work. I'll make us dinner."

"Wow! We're diving right into this, huh?"

"If you're already busy—"

"No, no," Lucy interrupted. "I don't have any plans. I'm not the one who keeps secrets." The latter was said with heavy condescension.

"Ha, ha. Look, I must go to the store before it closes, so I'll see you tomorrow. Is there anything special you want me to get?" Lee asked as she stood up and kissed her sister on the cheek.

"No, I'm good with anything, I'm not picky with food. Kind of like you with men." Lucy smiled sarcastically.

"Alright you brat drop it! Remember, *be nice*. Scott's very important to me," Lee said as she opened the door to leave.

She turned and gave Lucy a pleading look.

"Promise me you'll try to make this work! I love you, Luce."

"Uh, yeah. I promise, or whatever. Love you too."

And with that, Lee rushed out the door, squashing the potential for the conversation to go south, and smiling ear-to-ear at her incredible luck. She just hoped Lucy meant what she said.

***

"Wow, you look amazing!" Lee exclaimed as Lucy came through the door the next day. Lucy had donned a pale pink and red flower-patterned summer dress, complete with red lipstick and long fake eyelashes. She looked more like she was going out with her own boyfriend rather than meeting Lee's.

"Why thank you, dear sister. You could look this good too, you know," Lucy said jokingly.

"Except you know how much I don't like dresses or fake accessories because I can't handle seeing my own eyelashes," Lee said, gesturing to her eyes. "I swear I can feel a breeze every time you blink."

Lee was always as casual as she could get away with. She would rather be comfortable than couture. Lucy would call her lazy, teasing that she was sure if they scrolled through the photos on *peopleofwalmart.com*, Lee would be in there. This, of course, was an overstatement; Lee just preferred the more natural look. Plainer clothes that fit comfortably, and minimal to no makeup. Simple. Easy-peasy.

"Well, it's about time! I'm so glad to finally meet you," Scott said as he emerged from the kitchen wearing an apron over his jeans and black Metallica T-shirt. Lucy smiled and offered her hand, but he ignored it and went straight for a hug. Lucy stiffened but gave him a gentle pat on the back while maintaining her smile.

"It's a pleasure to meet you too, Scott. I'm sure you wouldn't have had to wait so long if I had known about you before yesterday," Lucy said sarcastically.

"I apologize," Scott said. "That's my fault. Lee just wanted to make sure I was worth introducing you to and not a waste of your time. I waited too long to propose. I should have done it when I knew she was the one."

"And when was that?" Lucy asked, stealing a surprised glance at Lee.

"About three days, five conversations, and one kiss after I met her." Scott smiled and pecked Lee on the cheek. "Now if you'll excuse me, I need to get back to the kitchen before anything burns."

The moment Scott disappeared into the kitchen, Lucy turned on Lee. She had the look of a panther about to pounce on its prey.

"About *three days, five conversations, and one kiss after I met her*," Lucy said, mimicking Scott, and then she pretended to gag.

Lee made a shushing motion and scowled at her.

"Proposed? Is that what you meant by 'not going anywhere?'" Lucy hissed.

Lee was silent. She had kind of botched the whole engagement reveal by being a chicken. Too nervous to tell Lucy on her own, and too embarrassed to tell Scott she was nervous.

"I thought you were making dinner?" Lucy added. "Since when do the men you date know what a stove is?"

"Look, I'm sorry I didn't tell you about the ring. But I did say he was important to me." Lee paused and took a deep breath. "He wanted to make a good first impression. And he's a fabulous cook. I just hope you can appreciate how much of an effort he's making." Lee looked at her sister sternly and folded her arms.

"Yes, yes. I always appreciate food I don't have to cook. And, fine! He gets a point for knowing his way around a kitchen. Now get me a glass of wine. White, if you have it," Lucy said, waving her hand dismissively at Lee. "And for Pete's sake," she continued, "would you relax? I promised I would be nice, so quit looking like I'm about to break your favourite toy. Let's have a glass of wine, eat good food, and have some pleasant conversation."

Lucy sounded mostly genuine, so Lee allowed herself a glimmer of hope.

***

Lee had elegantly laid out the table with her best dinnerware for the occasion, but the main attraction was, hands down, the food. Scott had prepared an aromatic adventure of chicken cordon bleu, jasmine rice, and steamed herbed vegetables. Lucy looked genuinely impressed. When they were finished, they moved to the living room, where Scott poured the remainder of the wine in their glasses.

"So, what was it like growing up a twin?" He directed the question at Lucy. "I'm a single child, so I have a hard time imagining having a sibling, let alone one that looks exactly like me."

"Oh…the stories we could tell, hey Lee?" Lucy teased. "Did you tell him about the dance?"

Lee giggled and shook her head.

"We were fourteen," Lucy began. "The only way we could go to the dance was if we got good enough grades. Of course, mine were a little below acceptable, but I wasn't upset since I had no interest in going anyway…until I found out James Case, my crush, was going. I begged Lee to trade places with me so I could go."

"You hid all my CDs and threatened to burn them until I agreed," Lee amended.

"Okay, so I was a tad dramatic. Anyway," Lucy swung her attention back to Scott. "I'll admit acting all sweet and shy while Dad was giving me the 'talk' about boys was difficult," Lucy laughed. "But the hardest part was getting James to notice me dressed in Lee's boring clothes!"

"Are you kidding me? The hardest part was convincing Dad I was you," Lee countered. "Pretending to be mad and ignoring him by sitting in your room all night was exhausting. I passed the time reading your diary."

Scott and Lucy laughed.

"Well, James was putty in my hands, especially since he thought I was the unconquerable twin," Lucy said. "Lee was a bit of a prude until you were, what, twenty?"

Lee shook her head with a smile.

"Yeah, that made for an awkward Monday. Poor guy got so embarrassed not knowing which twin he had been with that he avoided us like the plague. And I don't think Dad ever found out, did he?"

"I never told him," Lucy confirmed. "But I'm sure he knows now, wherever he is."

The mood sobered a little and Scott cleared his throat.

"Lee told me about your dad's passing. That's rough, losing your only parent so young, and not getting a chance to know your mom. It's nice to see you two doing so well when life dealt you a shit hand," Scott said earnestly.

Lucy shrugged and crinkled her nose.

"Yeah, I suppose we turned out alright. Dad told us lots of stories about what our mother was like. He made sure we knew that although she'd died in childbirth, it didn't mean it was our fault, and if she had to choose between her life and her babies, she wouldn't have hesitated to give hers up. We go to visit her grave every year."

Lucy paused briefly, and the corners of her mouth twitched.

"Now, the day Dad died was one of the best and worst days I've ever had."

Lee nodded in agreement.

"We had both graduated university that day and had gone to our favourite park for a picnic. We sat in the grass eating blueberry pie, feeding the birds, and I remember a lot of laughing. It was a good day. Then on the walk home, Dad started sweating and complaining of chest pain."

Lucy fell silent, and noticed Lee looking sombre. She changed the subject and gently patted Lee's arm.

"That's all behind us, though. Now we have a wedding to look forward to!"

At that, Lee looked up at Scott and smiled.

***

After Lucy had left, Lee collapsed on the couch with a satisfied sigh at how well the dinner had gone. Scott squeezed in beside her.

"So, where's that crazy, rude person you've been warning me about for the past year?" he asked.

"Oh, just you wait. She's in there! You got the charming, flirty, make-a-good-first-impression Lucy, so you still need to err on the side of caution. I will admit, though, she put on a stellar performance, and I'm grateful for it. Makes me feel like she cares."

"Maybe you should give her the benefit of the doubt; she does seem to genuinely care. I mean, why wouldn't she be happy for you? I am freaking amazing!" he said, donning a large, goofy smile. Lee giggled and cuddled up to him.

"I guess I could try to be more optimistic and allow the potential for growth on her part. I'm not holding my breath, though," Lee said shifting her weight to face him. "And for the record, it takes amazing to attract amazing, in case you didn't know."

"I love amazing," he said, leaning in for a kiss.

***

"Lucy's coming over soon, so put your pants on!" Lee said as she passed Scott in the hall, reaching out to pinch his butt cheek. His reluctance to wear anything but briefs when he stayed over was in a way adorable, but a little annoying when people came by and he had to scramble to the bedroom before she could open the door.

"Just for a visit, or a specific reason?" he asked as he pulled a pair of sweatpants on.

"Birthday plans. I know it's still three months away, but I have to book early if she agrees to my idea."

"What's your idea? Am I allowed to be involved this time?" Scott asked.

Lee could tell he still felt a little sore when she hadn't told him about her birthday the previous year. She'd felt guilty, but it was an immensely personal day for twins, and it always had been.

"Look, I'm sorry I didn't tell you last year, but Lucy wasn't aware of '*us*' then. We spent the morning at the grave site and the rest of the day at the racetrack placing expensive bets on shitty horses. You honestly didn't miss anything exciting. Besides, I need to ease Lucy into the idea of sharing that day with someone else. I planned to start talking to her about it after the wedding. So maybe this year we can do something just the two of us when I get back? Are you cool with that?"

Scott shrugged. "Yeah, I'm cool that. I get it: twins are weird."

Lee smirked.

"I can't even argue that."

A few moments later, Lucy stepped through the door while knocking, and before she could remove her shoes, Lee was waving the brochure in her face.

"Jesus, would you let me sit first? What is this?" Lucy demanded as she pulled the paper from Lee's hand, unfolding it as she made her way to the couch.

Lee bounced to her seat beside her and waited for the words to sink into Lucy's brain.

"Does this say Sunrise *Skydiving*?"

"*Yes!*" Lee squealed and clapped her hands. "I booked us in for the 1:00 p.m. jump. We have to be there by 11:00 a.m. to get through training. I need to put down a non-refundable deposit before they close today to guarantee our spot."

Lucy shook her head and stammered a bit. "I-I really don't want to do this."

"Why not? It's exciting!" Lee beamed.

"It's suicide," Lucy deadpanned.

Lee grabbed the laptop and started browsing the websites photos.

"Look. They've been doing this for years. See all the happy, *alive* faces? Not one dead body."

"I went with my buddies a couple years ago to that same place, Lucy," Scott added from the kitchen. "It's scary and incredible at the same time. Do it!"

"It's too expensive. I can't afford it. Besides, we always go to see Mom and Dad in the morning. It's a two-hour drive and this place is an hour in the opposite direction."

Lucy set the brochure down in a finalizing gesture, but Lee wasn't giving up that easy.

"I thought we could go after the dive and take a bit of a picnic, maybe make a bonfire. Also, I can pay. It will be my gift to you." Lee paused and smiled as sweetly as she could.

Lucy stared at Lee, looking suspicious. Danger was not Lee's normal, and for once in their life it was Lucy's turn to be on edge.

"I guess if you're paying, it'll be more like murder than suicide," Lucy reasoned.

"Awesome. I'm going to send the deposit before you change your mind." Lee paused for a moment. "I can't believe I'm doing this either, but I honestly feel it will be good for us to climb way the hell out of our comfort zones. My credit card is in my room—I'll go call it in."

Lee scooted to her bedroom with her phone. She was literally vibrating with excitement and anxiety, trying to keep her voice from shaking as she read out her card number to the young female assistant. *Oh God! What have I done?* she thought as she hung up the phone.

As she made her way back down the hall, Lee could hear Lucy whispering, but she couldn't quite make out what she was saying. She entered the kitchen to see Scott doing the dishes and Lucy drying them, which was an odd sight because Lucy *never* helped Lee with dishes. They were talking in low tones and Lucy was giggling. Lee wanted the two of them to get along, but something inside of her clenched unhappily. It only took Lee a second to figure out what: Lucy's *giggle*. It was her token flirty giggle, and Lee knew that sound well.

"It's confirmed! We are jumping out of a plane," Lee interrupted before she let her imagination get away completely.

"Yay," Lucy said in a flat voice as she dropped the dish towel on the counter. "That reminds me, I'm out of booze and should hit the liquor store. I'll talk to you later," she said in Lee's direction as she put her shoes on. Then she looked to Scott and added, "And you sooner."

"What did she mean by that?" Lee asked Scott the moment Lucy was out the door.

"She ordered a new love seat and needs help hauling it up the stairs to her apartment. It's being dropped off tomorrow, so I said I'd help." Scott shrugged and started draining the sink.

Lee shook her head a little. It was weird. Lucy never asked for help. "Why can't the people dropping it off take it upstairs?" she asked him.

"I'm not sure. I didn't ask. I just thought that since I have the day off, I would be nice and help out."

Scott furrowed his brow a bit and looked at Lee sideways. "Am I not supposed to help your sister?"

"No, no! Of course it's fine," Lee replied. "It's only a little strange, is all." She let out a small sigh and looked up at him as she slid an arm around his back. "Just please be careful with her. You still haven't witnessed her true 'glory,' and I don't want you to get hurt or caught in the middle of one of her puppet shows."

"Honey, I think you're overreacting. It's a piece of furniture. Ten minutes, and I'll be out of there," he said with a reassuring smile, kissing her forehead.

***

The following day, Lee was running late after work so she asked Scott to meet her for dinner instead of waiting to make something at home. Giorgio's was her favourite restaurant for pasta, and that was exactly what she was craving. She arrived first and ordered a red wine while she waited, pondering over the menu because she was too hungry to make just one choice. When Scott arrived one glass of wine later, she immediately knew something was wrong. He looked jittery: very much unlike his usual relaxed demeanour. He gave her a quick peck on the lips and sat down across from her.

"You feeling okay?" she asked right away.

"Of course! I'm fine," Scott said quickly as he picked up his menu. The waitress came over, took his drink order, then left to fill it while Scott kept flipping through pages.

"Spill it," Lee said.

"It's that obvious?" he asked.

"Painfully."

He put down the menu.

"Look, I didn't want to start anything. There's no reason for anyone to get upset because nothing happened." He fell quiet as the waitress returned with his drink and took their food order. Once she was gone, Lee folded her arms and waited for him to resume.

"I went to Lucy's to help with the love seat. Everything was fine at first. We got the thing upstairs, no issues, and it was actually pretty light. But once we were inside her place she started asking me to move stuff and, I don't know, looking at me funny. I don't know how to describe it, but I got really uncomfortable. Then she shut the door, which I found a little weird because I wasn't planning on staying. Anyway, I moved a couple things and made for the door while trying to be as polite as possible, but she grabbed my hand in a *weird* way. Then..."

Scott stopped and looked up at Lee, who was quietly and calmly listening. She made a rolling motion with her hand for him to go on, so he did.

"I can't be sure of what she was trying to do with my hand, but I jerked it away and stammered a 'see ya later' as I bolted out the door. Like I said, nothing happened. It was just incredibly awkward."

Lee pondered this a moment. She wasn't shocked, but she felt a little sad. She and Lucy had been getting along…she had hoped that Scott's presence in both their lives was a good thing. That hope was fading.

"What do you think she was trying to do with your hand?" she asked sincerely.

"Well, don't take this as fact, because I'm just guessing, but it seemed like…you know…she was coming onto me." Scott grimaced and shook his head. "Look, I'm not going to sit here and stir the pot between you two, but I'll be honest. The fact that she looks like you, but is not you, really messed with my head for a moment. I'm sorry I didn't listen, and I promise I will never go there without you again."

He reached across the table, offering his hand. She took it, trusting every word, reassuring him with a tight smile and a hand squeeze. She felt responsible for Lucy's behaviour; she always had.

"I'm the sorry one," she said. "I had a feeling something like this might happen. She's very competitive and controlling. Although, I swear sometimes she does stuff like this just to be wicked," Lee said acridly. "I'll talk to her, but I can't promise better behaviour. The only thing I can promise when it comes to Lucy is to expect the unexpected. She will deliver, and it's rarely good."

Lee sighed and propped her chin in the palm of her free hand.

"If at any point you felt like this was too much for you to handle, you would tell me, right?" Lee asked, half-hoping he wouldn't answer. This was the first relationship she had ever wanted to keep, and the thought of her own sister sabotaging it was completely breaking her heart. If she lost Scott, she honestly didn't know what she would do.

"I want to marry you," Scott said. "No matter what happens, we will work it out together. Your sister doesn't scare me."

***

Lucy was waiting for Lee in the lobby of her office building after a particularly bad day of work. It had been a couple weeks since Lee had last seen her, and it really didn't feel like it had been long enough. She hadn't confronted Lucy about her behavior with Scott last week. She was warring with the idea that it needed to be done but knowing how volatile her twin could be left Lee feeling exhausted and wanting to avoid the topic all together.

"Come shopping with me," Lucy said.

"Shopping for what?" Lee asked.

"Something sexy. I have important things to tell you!"

Lucy was wearing an "I know something you don't know" look on her face. As much as Lee wanted to simply tell her off and go home, she wouldn't make a scene at her workplace.

"Okay," Lee sighed. "The mall is a block away. Let's just walk."

***

"So, what are these important things you need to tell me?" Lee inquired as she grabbed a couple items to take to the change rooms. They'd been at the department store for almost an hour already and Lucy hadn't said much other than frivolous chatter.

"I met someone," Lucy blurted out.

Lee was so sure she had misheard her that she replayed a few different possibilities before she stalled out completely and just gawked at her.

Lucy continued without waiting for her to catch up. "I met him on a dating site. His name is Gabriel Shaw. He's a doctor and currently volunteering his services overseas." She laced the entire comment with smugness.

Lee finally snapped out of it. "Wow, Luce, that's great! Have you met him in person yet?"

"No, but we've chatted on the phone a few times in the last month. We're planning on meeting this weekend—hence the need for sexy things," she said, shaking a G-string.

Good. Maybe you'll leave my guy alone now, Lee thought.

"You are meeting in a safe place, right? You didn't give him your address or anything, did you?"

"I'm not stupid, Lee," Lucy snapped as they entered change rooms next to each other. "Give me some credit."

"Speaking of…" Lee said over the stall. She took a deep breath and made the dive. "What happened with Scott when he helped you with the love seat?"

"What do you mean?" her sister responded, voice muffled, cloth rustling on the other side of the partition.

Lee waited a moment before responding. "Well…he got the impression you were hitting on him."

Lucy laughed, sharp and abrupt. It wasn't a nice sound. Lee heard her sister's change room door open and when Lucy spoke again, it was from the bank of mirrors along the far wall.

Lee opened her change room door too and said nothing as her twin twisted one way, then the other in the long mirrors. Finally, Lucy looked at her and said in a snotty tone, "Look, I have no idea where he got that idea from, but I think Scotty needs to get over himself. No offence, dear sister, but he's not my type."

"So…nothing awkward happened?" Lee pressed, watching her twin's face carefully.

Lucy turned away from the mirrors and faced her.

"No! Who are you going to believe? Some guy you've barely known a year, or the twin you shared a womb with?"

"Okay, okay. I'll drop it," Lee said. She didn't feel like fighting and was hoping this doctor guy was real enough to keep Lucy occupied for a while.

They each picked a piece to purchase and headed for the till. Lee was a little surprised to see Lucy holding onto a blue satin set since her go-to colour was almost always red, but she didn't say anything.

"By the way, I saw Scott yesterday sitting outside that cafe you like," Lucy said nonchalantly over her shoulder. "He wasn't alone. She was very pretty."

Lee rolled her eyes at the back of Lucy's head.

"I know, Luce. That was his cousin. She's starting school in the fall, and he was showing her around."

"Oh thank goodness. I'm just looking out for you," Lucy said in an uncaring tone.

Lee was so annoyed she thought of just dropping her black lace and walking away.

"You two doing anything for the rest of the week?" Lucy asked.

"Nothing planned but work. I'm swamped and will definitely be working late until the weekend," Lee replied flatly.

"Is Scott okay with you working so much?"

Jesus, as if she really cares.

"He's been pretty busy too. We haven't caught up on each other's schedules because we're not always sure what they are. We both have the weekend off, so I'll touch base with him then…" Lee's voice trailed off when it became apparent her sister wasn't listening anyway.

Lucy finished her payment and turned to Lee.

"I'll tell you how it goes," she said, shaking her purchase at her.

"Can't wait!" Lee lied and watched Lucy strut out of the store.

***

"Give me a minute to freshen up," Lee yelled from Scott's en-suite bathroom as she yanked off her clothes to inspect the new black lace lingerie she donned underneath. It had been a few days since they had seen each other, and she was eager to show it off. Nothing destressed a busy week quite like good sex, and she could hardly wait to get relaxed.

"Ready when you are," Scott said, and she opened the door for the reveal.

Scott stared at her hungrily.

"You are the most beautiful woman I've ever known. How much lingerie did you buy?" Scott asked.

Lee furrowed her brow a bit at the question but maintained her smile.

"What do you mean?" she asked.

"Can I take pictures again?" he asked, ignoring her question as he grabbed his phone off the nightstand and approached her.

"Look how beautiful you are," he added as he handed her his phone.

Lee stared in growing horror at the impossible photos.

"I really liked the blue satin, but this is hands-down amazing."

Scott returned to the bed, beckoning for her to come to him, but Lee was frozen. Her mind was reeling as images of Lucy in a blue satin two-piece swiped across the screen of Scott's phone… Lucy posing for him, kissing him, going down on him… photos of her twin on *her* fiancé's phone!

Lee closed her eyes. *Oh my God.* She couldn't look anymore and she quickly tossed the phone in the direction of the bed. She began wiping her hand on her leg as if to rid it of the filth it had held.

"Are you okay?" Scott asked and Lee was jerked from her tormented reverie.

"I-I don't feel well," Lee stammered, turning back into the bathroom. She frantically began pulling her clothes back on. She could hear Scott rise from the bed and approach the en-suite's door. Lee kept her face down, hair sliding forward to hide her devastated features.

"Honey, what are you doing? A minute ago you were ready to jump my bones and now you look… really upset. Is it the pictures? Are you embarrassed? Because you shouldn't be."

He paused to give her a chance to respond but she didn't even look his direction.

"Look, if you're honestly sick, you should stay. I'll take care of you," he added.

"No, I don't want to throw up in front of you yet," Lee said quickly. She could barely get the words out without her voice cracking. All she could focus on was leaving before the tears came. She pushed past Scott, grabbed her purse and hurried for the door.

"Lee, please, I don't understand what just happened here," Scott pleaded.

"I'll be fine," she said firmly as she reached the door. "I'll call you later. I love you."

Lee turned and ran down the stairs as a flood of hot, angry tears flowed down her cheeks.

***

I can't believe this is happening, it can't be real. How could she? How could he not notice? Why?

Lee pulled into a vacant parking lot, parked the SUV and rolled the window down, sucking in deep breaths of the cool night air.

She cut and coloured her hair like mine, she chose blue because that's what I normally buy, and she even asked what our plans were...

She wiped her eyes to clear her vision and let out a sob. Her mind continued to reel. Scott. He had obviously been clueless but that didn't make it feel like less of a betrayal from him. As soon as the thought entered her mind, Lee flung it out. No, that wasn't fair. He hadn't known, how could he? He had no idea the level of shit Lucy could shovel at someone.

Hell I didn't even expect this.

If he knew it had been Lucy, he'd be devastated. He'd leave and once again, she'd be alone. With her. Lee wiped her tears and muttered aloud, "Not this time dear sister..."

She started on her way again without consciously choosing a direction. She was too angry to think straight, too hurt to deal with another human but ready to dance with the devil. That's when she realized she had pulled into Lucy's parking lot.

Lee barged in without knocking and slammed the door behind her.

"How could you?" Lee ground out, shaking with rage.

Lucy was sitting calmly on the couch.

"So, are you mad that I fucked him? Or mad that he couldn't tell the difference?"

There is such a thing as blackout rage. Lee honestly did not remember lunging across the room or jumping on her sister. She could not recall punching and scratching Lucy's face until her hands ached and throbbed with fire. She couldn't recount the obscenities she screamed at her. What she did remember was the sight of her sister lying at her feet, hands covering her bloody face. A wave of guilt and horror washed over her as she watched Lucy's quaking shoulders, until she realized that what she thought was sobbing was laughter, maniacal laughter that followed her out the door and down the street.

***

Over six weeks had passed since that night. Lee had to admit it was far less stressful without Lucy around, but a feeling of not being quite "whole" lingered. Until the pictures flashed across her memory, that is; then she felt more murderous than empty. She had deleted them, much to Scott's dismay, but she promised to get professional boudoir photos done to appease him.

Poor Scott. Lee still hadn't told him. She struggled with this every day, but the thought of losing him killed her. He knew the twins had had a blowout and he had his suspicions, but Lee only gave enough to ease his curiosity, nothing concrete. The one thing Lee was sure of? Scott would leave if he learned the truth, and then Lucy would win. But she felt stuck. Like she was in a Mexican standoff where no one could proceed or retreat without risking everything.

Until she saw the letter.

Sometime, in the early hours of a Sunday morning, an envelope had been slipped under Lee's door, and she knew instantly it was Lucy. She took a deep breath as she opened it, quickly skimming the lines.

Dear Sister,

I'm sorry. I realize I may have gone a tad overboard. I don't know what came over me. Jealousy, I guess. Anyway, I feel bad, and I miss you. Our birthday is coming up, and I still want to spend it with you like we always have. I can't imagine going to the graveyard alone. Besides, didn't you say the skydiving deposit was non-refundable? Might as well go. I'll even let you push me out of the plane!

Love you,
Lucy

When Lee was done she crumpled it up and threw it in the garbage.

"She still wants to be together on our birthday," she told Scott later that morning. "I'm so sorry, yadda, yadda, yadda, Mom and Dad's grave visit blah, blah, non-refundable skydiving deposit. Ugh," she finished, shoulders slumped and staring off into space

"I think you should go," Scott said.

Lee raised her eyebrows and looked at him as if he was crazy.

"I'm serious. I think you should go," he said. "You haven't been yourself at all since your huge fight with her. You're quieter, distant. I know you don't want to talk about it with me, but you need to resolve whatever happened with her."

Lee sat quietly, reflecting for a moment before deciding he was right. As much as she despised Lucy, she was still her twin, and Lee deserved some answers. She sighed.

"Okay, I'll go."

***

The ride out was awkward for Lee. Lucy was chatting away like nothing had happened and all was forgiven simply because Lee agreed to go through with their plans. Lee was still having a hard time looking at her twin, contributing the odd one-word response because she was only half-listening.

When they arrived at the small private airfield, they were greeted by a couple of tanned, long haired surfer-looking young men. They signed their lives away on agreement waivers and started their training. The twins were paired up with their tandem partners and tried a couple practice jumps from a wooden prop. Lee was secretly hoping Lucy's harness would fail.

By the time the training was done, threatening clouds had rolled in and delayed the jump time. Lee took the opportunity to get to know her partner a little better, seeing as her life was in his hands.

It took a while, but the skies finally cleared. As they readied themselves to board the plane Lucy turned to Lee and joked, "Last chance to back out! Should I be checking my harness?"

"Let's do this!" Lee said with a fake smile. Truth be told, she *was* getting excited for the jump and was glad to be there, present company excluded.

Her nerves really hit her once they reached altitude, but it all went so fast she didn't have time to build a solid healthy fear and let her self-preservation instincts make her stay in the plane.

Lee went first. She swung her legs out and had three whole seconds to reflect on her life decisions before she found herself hurtling towards the ground. The wind was deafening. Her instructor was spinning them like a top. Lee squeezed her eyes shut and screamed like a child on a fair ride. After what seemed like an eternity, they straightened out and he yelled at her to pull the cord. There was a whoosh of ruffling fabric, and instantly the world became quiet and calm. Lee slowly opened her eyes and gasped at the world from her newfound angle. The green fields, the rolling hills so immense from the ground now looked as if she could scoop it all up in her arms. Like she could literally hold the world in her hands. She could see for endless miles all around her, and it was truly breathtaking. It was true serenity, something she had not felt in months, perhaps even years and she savoured it not knowing if she would ever feel it again.

They gently floated in silence as Lee took in as much of the experience as she could. She hadn't felt this alive and free in a very long time. Once they had landed (half-running, half-stumbling) and taken off the harnesses, Lee turned and hugged her instructor in thanks. Lucy was laughing as she approached them.

"Oh my God, Lee! That was amazing! I almost pissed myself," she said as she threw her arms around her. Lee cringed a bit on the inside but gave her a small hug in return.

Oh to hell with it, Lee thought. *This is the last day I'll ever spend with her again, so maybe I could afford some high points and let some of this anger go.*

"We need to stop at my place so I can grab a couple things for the graveyard," Lucy said.

***

Lee pulled the SUV up to Lucy's apartment, and Lucy jumped out.

"I'll be right back," she said and jogged to the entrance.

Lee sat for a moment, thinking about the two-hour drive to the family plot and her bladder reminded her that it was a long trip. She decided to run in and use Lucy's washroom but when Lee opened the door to Lucy's apartment, she was dumbstruck. The place was completely empty. No furniture, no pictures, no boxes. Lucy came out of the bedroom with a large bag and looked at her sister, her expression growing sheepish.

"I was going to tell you later," Lucy said. "Gabriel asked me to move in with him. I don't have a whole lot going on here. No career, no friends. So I thought, why not! I sold—or threw out—all my stuff, quit my job, and I leave tomorrow."

Lee was utterly surprised. And utterly thankful. She said nothing as she approached Lucy and gave her sister a genuine hug.

***

With empty bladders and loaded provisions, they made the yearly trek to visit their parents. Their uncle had owned the old family farm south of the city in what was quite literally the middle of nowhere. He had passed with no immediate family to leave it to and no will. In the end the land was bought by the bank and rented out to local farmers. In the middle of that land was their old family graveyard, the last two plots taken by their parents.

By the time they got a fire going and lawn chairs set up, night had fallen. Lee sat admiring the colour of the flames dancing in front of her, thinking about Lucy's departure and how it eased her mind about her own future. She felt much more at peace with her plans now.

Lucy produced the bag she'd packed and pulled out a bottle of wine and two cups. She also, much to Lee's surprise, pulled out a pie and started cutting pieces for the two of them.

"Is that blueberry?" Lee asked.

"Of course!" Lucy replied. "Baked it myself this morning."

"Like the one you made for us that last day we had with Dad," Lee stated wistfully, appreciating the sentiment.

"Exactly like that one," Lucy replied with a smile and handed her a piece.

Lee finished her pie quickly. It had a bitter taste to it, but she didn't want to hurt Lucy's feelings. Lucy was trying to be nice, and Lee didn't want to spoil it. She finished her wine and grabbed the bottle for a refill.

"So, what have you been up to the past month?" Lucy asked.

"Actually, kind of the same as you," Lee confessed. "Scott and I are moving. An opportunity came up for me for a transfer to a new office. Scott can practice anywhere we go, so…"

Lee waited for her sister's usual, explosive reaction, but none came.

"Where are you guys going?" Lucy asked.

Lee hesitated and said nothing, feeling her cheeks redden as she looked the ground.

"Oh, I see." Lucy said flatly. "You're not going to tell me."

"I can't risk this," Lee said finally. "I love Scott and I'm not letting you ruin it. Besides, you'll be busy saving lives with Doctor Gabe, right?"

Lucy downed her wine and poured herself another.

"How will I find you, if I need you?"

Lee shrugged and stared at the fire.

"Really?" Lucy snapped. "You're completely shutting me out? I'm your twin sister!"

"Yes!" Lee snapped back, her voice rising. "Yes. I'm shutting out the *twin* who slept with my fiancé just to hurt me! What kind of *sister* does that?"

Lee stood abruptly and walked the short distance to her parents' graves. She needed a moment to try and dispel her anger. She still had to drive home with the witch.

Lucy unexpectedly kept quiet and let Lee have her moment to stare into the dark. The pit in Lee's stomach was starting to feel less like anxiety and more like a cramp. In fact, she was feeling queasy and a little hot.

"What's the matter?" Lucy said when Lee finally turned around. She had an odd expression on her face. "You don't look so good."

"I want to go," Lee said as she returned to the fire. "I'm not feeling so great."

Lucy made no motion to get up and instead, poured herself another drink. She drank it in three long swallows and wiped her mouth with the back of her hand.

Lee stood, her stomach aching, waiting for Lucy to say her piece when her eyes fell on the leftover pie. There was only one piece gone.

"How could you choose him?" Lucy said.

"What do you mean?"

Lucy stood up, taking a swig straight from the bottle. "How the fuck could you choose a man over me? I don't get you! *I'm your twin sister*. That's supposed to be special. It's supposed to mean something more."

A sad look spread over Lucy's face and she paused for a moment. "I just never understood why you were always so eager to leave. First Dad, now Scott..." She trailed off and went quiet.

Lee didn't understand at first, but then she remembered how her father had pushed her to take a job in Hawaii after graduation. She'd never left though because he had died.

Lee's eyes went back to the pie then down at her trembling hands and she realized how badly she was sweating as a wave of painful cramping seized her stomach.

"Why didn't you eat any of the pie, Luce?" Lee asked as the cold realization gripped her. "What did you do?"

"What I had to," Lucy said with a smile. "Dad was trying to separate us. I couldn't let that happen. But after he died, I couldn't believe how lucky I was to not get caught. Your stupid boyfriends were easy to get rid of, but I could tell Scott was different. It took me a while, but I realized the harder I try to reel you in, the further you drift away. That's when it hit me. I'm not happy on my own, so if I can't keep you, *maybe I can be you.*"

Lee's mind was reeling, and so were her insides. She leaned over the side of her chair and retched.

Lucy giggled. "It's too late for that," she said.

Lee bolted for the SUV. But as she reached for the door she heard the sound of jingling behind her. Lucy had the keys, the fire between them, casting a glow that made her look even more sinister. Lee stepped back away from the SUV and faced Lucy.

"What's in the pie, Lucy?"

"Belladonna," she confirmed, then took another long pull from the bottle.

Lee grimaced.

"That's the real reason you slept with Scott—to see if he would know the difference. The doctor isn't real, is he?"

"Ding, ding! No one looks for a body if they don't suspect you're dead," Lucy chimed with pride.

"Dad..." Lee started but couldn't finish as tears started to roll down her cheeks. She staggered a bit before catching herself. *I need those keys,* she thought as her eyes fell once again to the pie. Only this time she focused more on the knife used to cut it.

Lee began inching her way around the fire towards her sister. Lucy didn't seem to notice. In fact, she looked relaxed and confident that she had all her bases covered. Lee took a couple steps closer, careful not to look at her target and raise suspicion.

"You should just sit down and try to relax, Lee. Really, the more you struggle the worse it will be," Lucy said with an irritatingly worried tone. She gestured for Lee to sit and so, Lee sat.

In Lucy's chair.

Within arm's reach of the knife.

Her heart was racing, and she had never been so scared and enraged in all her life.

Lucy inspected what was left in the bottle in her hand and took one last swallow. When she looked back at Lee, she was standing less than a foot away, their eyes locked in an icy glare despite the beads of sweat. Lucy's demeanour took on a more serious note even before she noticed the firelight glinting off the steel blade gripped in Lee's hand.

Lucy realized she had drank too much. She staggered slightly and tightened her fingers around the neck of the empty bottle.

"We don't have time for this," Lee said, then raised the knife.

***

She stole a glance at the skull's empty sockets where blue eyes had once gleamed.

"You know, I honestly thought life would be easier without you in it. It doesn't feel easier. I've been struggling in silence, unable to talk about what happened. I know they say time heals everything, but every day I feel more and more...alone," she said, staring off into the darkness.

"You're probably wondering about Scott. Well, we're together, but I don't think it's going to last much longer to be honest. He can tell I'm not the same. How could I be..." She trailed off and took another sip.

"A part of myself died here. I didn't go back whole. I doubt I'll ever feel like a complete person again," she said as she gazed up at the split tree with empathy. Dead and rotting because of separation.

She took a moment to admire the distant stars and listen to the leaves rustle in the night air. Then she stood and began gathering her things. She looked down at her dead sister.

"Happy birthday," she said sadly as she stood and started to walk back to the SUV. She passed her parents' graves without looking at them, afraid of the judgement and shame. The air became heavy, the smell of earth more pungent, and the night seemed to grow a little darker. She shivered and turned around to give her sister's remains one last look when she thought she heard a familiar voice float by on the cold breeze: *"Dear sister."*

THE INCIDENT IN MILLS

"The little hamlet of Mills, Saskatchewan, is an isolated community with a population of about three hundred people and is surrounded by a dense boreal forest that stretches for hundreds of miles in every direction. The town has an automotive garage, one hotel restaurant-and-bar combination, and a small convenience store. It is the perfect stop for the nature enthusiasts. Mills is best known as the home of Saskatchewan's famous Mills Homestyle Fries.

Thick-cut russet red potatoes, seasoned to perfection and deep-fried to a flawless golden crisp. Their claim to fame? The hint of bacon flavour found in the cooking oil: a traditional family secret."

JULY 2002

CINDY CAMERON CLOSED THE BOOK. She'd received *Small Towns of Saskatchewan* from her sister as a birthday gift. The eight-hour drive to her see her parents last week had given her the perfect opportunity to read it. The flat tire that had them sitting on the side of the highway just south of Mills had given her the opportunity to provide her family with a fun, educational tidbit.

The glare she got from her husband suggested he didn't find it as enlightening as Cindy did. He pulled on the tire wrench as hard as he could, but the lug nuts on the Escalade didn't budge a millimetre. He let out an oath of frustration as he threw the wrench to the shoulder of the road.

"Jason," Cindy admonished as she glanced into the vehicle. "Language, please."

Their thirteen-year-old daughter Mandy was busy on her tablet, earbuds in, oblivious to the world. Pebbles, their miniature poodle, lay curled up beside her.

Jason said as much as he rose to his feet, swiping at the black flies that swarmed around him. They didn't seem to be bothering Cindy, and he felt an irrational stab of jealousy. He looked around, stared down at the lack of bars on his cell phone, and cursed again. God, he hated the country. Rural life would never be his first choice. Or his last. The shortcut he'd chosen to get them home an hour early had put them on a narrow highway, wrought with potholes and broken tarmac. The surrounding forest pressed in on both sides, thick and wildly overgrown. Jason shuddered. Who could possibly enjoy living out here?

"Well, I can't get this tire off," Jason said as he slapped the dirt from the knees of his designer jeans. "And we have no cell service. Get Mandy and the dog and let's start walking."

"What?" Cindy said, her blue eyes widening a little. "Walk? To where?"

Jason hooked a thumb at the sign for Mills.

"It's only ten kilometers," he said as he reached inside the Escalade for his wallet and the keys. "We run that every day. At least one of us still does."

Jason saw the hurt, then anger, flash across his wife's face, but he pretended not to. It was a mean thing to say, he knew that. Cindy had undergone surgery a few months earlier, and it had really cut into her time at the gym. But that had been three months ago already. He was pretty sure she could be doing something to stay in shape. *Mandy too*, he thought. She was short, a little chubby, and very self-conscious. She had cried last month when he had pointed out how poor her afternoon snack choices were.

"Eat the apple, ditch the cheese, kid!" he'd said and then pointed out that if she got into something worthwhile after school, like swimming or basketball instead of band and book club, she wouldn't be such a pudge ball.

When Cindy had heard that, it had led to a divorce-worthy fight. Jason knew that what he'd said to their daughter wasn't conducive to a healthy self-image, but he was starting to worry about her. Being a fat kid was not an easy way to grow up! He knew that firsthand. He'd literally worked his ass off to get the physique he had today. At forty-five, he still worked every day to make healthy choices, to exercise, and stay fit. It wasn't easy. Mandy wasn't even trying, and Cindy was letting her get away with it. Not to mention her own lackadaisical lifestyle, surgery or not.

They'd only walked for about ten minutes before a police car came over the hill and slowed to a stop beside them. Good thing, too. Mandy was lagging behind with Pebbles, and Cindy had expressed discomfort in her right knee on the very first hill.

One hill? Seriously? Jason had shaken his head and walked faster.

"Good afternoon," the officer greeted them.

Jason tried not to scoff at what he believed was the stereotypical-looking cop: short, fat, and bald with glasses perched on the end of his pug-like nose. He climbed out of the vehicle.

"What are you folks doing walking way out here?"

"Hello," Cindy greeted warmly as she hurried forward to shake the man's hand. His name tag read 'Constable Wagner.' "We had car trouble. A flat tire." She gestured to Jason and added, "He couldn't get the, uh, the things, to loosen off. You know?"

"The *lug nuts*," Jason emphasized the correct terminology, "are torqued on. Nobody can get those off without a torque wrench."

He was pleased at how knowledgeable he sounded even though he only knew that much because the salesman at the dealership had made the same comment when Jason had expressed concern over the gold-plated rims getting stolen.

Living in the city of Calgary afforded them the luxury of never having to worry about such things as flat tires; that's what insurance was for. But out here in the middle of nowhere-Saskatchewan…Jason rolled his shoulders and let out a huff of air.

"Anyway, it's at the corner, down the hill there," he said with a gesture.

Constable Wagner eyed him up and down, then smiled politely at Cindy and gestured to his squad car.

"I can radio for a tow. Have your vehicle brought to the garage in Mills."

"And will the staff there know anything about an Escalade?" Jason asked pointedly.

"They will know how to change a flat tire," Constable Wagner replied, giving him a polite smile that didn't quite reach his eyes. "Can give you a lift to the hotel if you like, too. It's got a restaurant. Food is simple but cheap."

Jason scowled at the condescending tone the older man had taken with him and opened his mouth to say so.

"Thank you!" Cindy jumped in. "That would be wonderful. Thank you very much."

Constable Wagner nodded and unlocked the vehicle's back doors.

"Besides," he said, "it's not safe walking these roads with a child and a little dog. There are plenty of creatures in these woods that would consider them a snack."

Cindy's smile faded and she beckoned Mandy closer to her. Mandy scooped up Pebbles, hugging the cinnamon-coloured dog tight to her chest as she glanced around the close-pressed woods.

"Yes, I heard the squirrels up here can be pretty aggressive," Jason said sarcastically as he headed for the front seat of the squad car.

Cindy kept up a running conversation with Constable Wagner after he radioed back to Mills to have the vehicle towed. They crested the last hill—Jason would never have admitted it out loud, but it would have been a difficult ten-kilometre hike—and began the descent. Potato fields stretched across the valley floor. They saw the occasional pasture with cattle and at one point they passed a game fence. It was heavily covered in brush and trees, but Jason thought he caught a glimpse of pale, pink-skinned pigs. He asked, and Constable Wagner confirmed with a nod.

"Schneider Pork Producers," Constable Wagner said when Jason asked about them. "Family-run farm. They tend to keep to themselves."

"I bet they do," Jason scoffed. "Christ, they must stink."

"Jason!" Cindy snapped.

"What?" he snapped back. "Pig farmers are disgusting! Don't you remember that truck and trailer we encountered outside Lethbridge last year? It reeked. And so did the people driving it. They were pig farmers."

"Wasn't that bad," Mandy muttered under her breath, and Jason turned in his seat to look back at her. The bullet-proof divider made her image look distorted and blurry. She stared at him, her chin lifted in defiance.

"My wife grew up on a hog farm down south," Constable Wagner said, guiding the car around a tight bend. "Her parents are retired millionaires. Worth a little bit of a stink, I'd say."

Jason pressed his lips together and tried not to smile as he stared out the passenger-side window. *No comment*, he thought to himself as Cindy bombarded Wagner with an onslaught of new questions.

They came to a wide, clear approach to a paved driveway. There was a big, black sign mounted atop a huge wrought-iron gate that announced the Mills Homestyle Fries plant. Jason peered past Constable Wagner as they drove by it.

Cindy nudged Mandy.

"Look, honey," she crooned, brushing a strand of Mandy's long blonde hair off her shoulder. "This is where they make your favourite French fries!"

Mandy looked up.

"Cool!" she said.

It was the most enthusiasm Jason had heard out of her in months.

"I bet *you* know what gives the fries their infamous flavour," Cindy teased Constable Wagner with a laugh.

He chuckled too and glanced in the rear-view mirror.

"Can't say," he teased back. "Trade secret."

"What? If you told us, you'd have to kill us?" Jason joked.

The older man gave him an oblique look.

"Somethin' like that," he rumbled.

***

The town of Mills was pretty much how Jason had imagined it: less than a one horse town, with cracked sidewalks and rundown buildings, most of which were boarded up and empty. He assumed most of the residents worked at the plant.

There were noticeably odd-looking individuals walking around looking weirdly alike with their pale skin, muddy brown hair, and lacklustre blue eyes that seemed to look through rather than at you. They all looked…related.

Typical small town, he thought. *Disgusting*.

Constable Wagner pulled up in front of a two-storey whitewashed building that had a blue sign announcing it as the Mills Hotel Restaurant and Bar. Three people walked past the car, staring at the newcomers as they got out. Like most of the people Jason had spotted as they'd driven into town, these three individuals looked like carbon copies of each other.

Jason wrinkled his nose and nudged Cindy.

"Inbreeding much?" he muttered.

"Jason!" she hissed angrily. "For God's sake!"

"I'll let you off here," said Constable Wagner. "Your truck will be towed up the street there, to the garage. Jamie Kersch is the owner. He'll look after you."

"Wonderful," Cindy said, giving the officer a genuine smile. "We appreciate all your help."

"Yeah, thanks," Jason added as he stared up and down the street. Mandy joined Cindy on the sidewalk, and they were starting for the front doors of the hotel when Wagner cleared his throat.

"Um, ma'am. Pardon me, but the dog," he said, and gestured to Pebbles. "They won't let her in the restaurant."

"Oh," Cindy said. "Right. How silly of me…"

"I'm not hungry," Mandy piped up, hugging the dog tightly. "I can wait out here with Pebbles. You guys go eat."

"That's a good idea," Jason said quickly. "Won't kill you to skip a meal, anyway."

He reached out with a teasing laugh and poked at his daughter's soft tummy.

Mandy spun away from them, her face reddening, and she buried it in the small dog's coat. Pebbles whined and squirmed, trying to wriggle around and lick her favourite human.

"*Jason!* That was out of line."

Cindy's tone was scathingly serious, and he made an exasperated gesture.

"Jesus!" he moaned. "I'm just kidding. Mandy, relax kid. I'm teasing you. I didn't mean…"

Constable Wagner gave Jason a very dark look as he shouldered past him and knelt in front of Mandy.

"Sweetheart, I can take Miss Pebbles over to the station with me."

He spoke in a gentle voice, his round face soft with compassion. He gestured to a squat, red brick building on the corner across the street.

"We have a big fenced-in yard out back with a picnic table where we like to sit and have coffee. She can play out there, and I will personally watch over her until you come pick her up."

Mandy's eyes were damp with tears when she looked at the rotund officer.

"You definitely don't need to skip a meal," Wagner continued. "You are too small for that! And it would be an absolute sin to be here in Mills and not have a plate of Homestyle Fries cooked up fresh for you. They are better than anything you get in the stores back home. I promise."

Mandy hesitated a second longer, then carefully passed Pebbles to him. Then she turned to her mom and headed for the restaurant, ignoring her father completely.

Jason glanced at the officer and shrugged.

"Women," he said. "They're so sensitive about their waistlines. Not like us, eh?"

Wagner stared at Jason for a beat, then shook his head and climbed back into the squad car. Pebbles stood happily on his lap, mouth open and tongue lolling in a doggy grin as her little paws balanced on the steering wheel.

***

Jason didn't know what had been worse: the limp salad, bland soup, and useless white bread sandwich he'd tried to eat, or watching his wife and daughter chow down on a heaping plate of fries and gravy, then tuck into oversized bowls of apple crisp with homemade butterscotch sauce. Regardless, he was grateful when it was over. He let the waitress know how poor his meal had been and fumed when Cindy and Mandy gushed over theirs. He paid. Cindy tipped. And he stalked out of the poor excuse for a restaurant.

They collected Pebbles—more gushing about the great food—and Jason left the women to their slower-paced ramble as he strode towards the oily-looking little garage down the street.

"God…if these rednecks get even a speck of anything on the Escalade, I am going to lose my mind," Jason muttered as he entered the garage.

It took a few minutes before someone arrived at the service counter; just long enough for Jason to get even more annoyed and for Mandy and Cindy to join him.

"The rim is bent," said the mechanic.

Jamie-what's-his-name was not around, and Jason scowled down at the shorter, rheumy-eyed young man. He looked just like everyone else in town, with his too-pale skin and lank, dishwater-coloured hair.

"No, it isn't," Jason snapped.

The mechanic wiped his greasy hands on an equally greasy towel.

"Yeah," he said firmly and nodded towards the truck. "It is. You musta' driven on it while it was flat for a while."

"No," Jason insisted firmly. "I did not."

"Umm…" Cindy said behind him, and he felt his brain start to sizzle with fury. "Actually, hon, you kind of did. I heard it blow, and it was a while before we pulled over. You were looking for cell service to call Triple A."

"Sure. Fine. Whatever," he snapped.

Insurance, he thought. *We have insurance for this crap.*

"How soon can you have it fixed? A couple of hours?"

"No, sir," the mechanic said firmly. "We have to get a new rim sent up from Saskatoon or Prince Albert. Should be here by tomorrow afternoon. Can likely get you on your way shortly after that."

"*Tomorrow afternoon?*" Jason exploded. "What the hell are we supposed to do until then?"

"Look, mister. It's the best we can do, unless you want to get your truck towed out of here. Either way, that ain't happening until tomorrow afternoon. So what do you want to do? I need to call the city and get the rim shipped up."

Jason raked his hands through his dark hair and planted them on his lean hips.

"Jesus," he muttered angrily. "Fine, fine. Get the rim shipped up. Then at least we can get out of this backward province."

The young mechanic just stared at him. "We'll call you tomorrow when your rim gets here. Leave your cell number at the front desk," he said and he walked away.

"Leave my number? There's no goddamn cell service here!" Jason snapped.

"It's a small town," Cindy said, and her voice was like ice. "There's one hotel. They will find us."

Jason glared daggers into her back as she and Mandy gathered whatever they could carry out of the Escalade. It looked like they were staying in Mills.

***

The hotel was old and smelled funny. The room had two double beds with barely enough room to walk between them. There was no way Jason was taking his shoes off. The carpet had to be a hundred years old, and who knew what had been ground into them over the years. Pebbles was paying way too much attention to a particular spot in the rug for his comfort. The windowpanes were grimy and looked out over the main street. The blinds were yellowed with age, and the bathroom…Jason shuddered.

"It's dated," Cindy said as she inspected the small rooms. "But everything looks clean."

He stared at her, aghast.

"What?" his wife snapped. "It's old, but it's clean. It even smells good in here."

"A-are you insane?" Jason sputtered. "It smells like your mother's house, and the tub and sink are practically rusted through!"

"Rust doesn't mean dirty, Jason! Jesus! When did you become such a snob?"

He started to argue, but she cut him off.

"And how dare you insult my mother's house!"

"Well, it stinks like old people," he muttered sullenly.

"That's not old people," she yelled. "It's called Pine-Sol! It's a floor cleaner, you insolent ass!"

Mandy gathered Pebbles up and left the room. He barely noticed as Cindy went up one side of him and down the other. Then she stalked out of the room too. Jason stood there for another moment before gingerly sitting down on the bed. He leaned over and cautiously sniffed the bedspread.

Okay, he thought, *maybe it does, mostly, smell like fabric softener. But still...*

Mandy and Cindy came back about an hour later. With ice cream cones.

Jason glanced up from the crappy little TV he'd been channel-surfing on and shook his head.

"Oh, good. That's a nice healthy snack before bed," he muttered. His stomach growled in disagreement, however.

Mandy slammed the door to the bathroom, Pebbles jumped up beside him and tried to lick his face—he gave her a cursory pat—and Cindy leaned in.

"Jason," she said quietly.

He looked at her. Her eyes were like granite, her expression deadly.

"If you ever fat shame our daughter again, I will divorce you and leave you penniless. Do you understand me? You are lucky to have us. I will not—"

Jason stood up.

Nightshades

"I'm not having this fight again," he said as he dug through the luggage and changed into a pair of jogging shorts and a T-shirt. He could feel Cindy's eyes burning holes in his back. "I'm going for a run."

He tromped downstairs, out the hotel door, and stood on the broken sidewalk as he stretched and shook his legs to limber up. He looked left, broken-down-town, weird people, and looked right. *The road leaving this craphole*, he thought, *looks infinitely more inviting.* Jason headed in that direction. At the end of the block, a man walked around the corner.

"Holy!" Jason squawked as he staggered backwards.

The man—and Jason was guessing it was a man simply because he had very short hair—was *huge*. He was massively, morbidly obese, and he was buck naked. Mounds of pale flesh jiggled in the evening sunlight, sweat-slicked and shiny. He waddled, arms out to the sides like some super-sized toddler. He was looking side-to-side, his dark eyes flicking constantly, and he was making painful grunting noises. Spittle ran from the corners of his mouth and his body heaved and wheezed as he struggled to breathe. A gust of wind sent a waft of air in Jason's direction, and he gagged as he backed rapidly away.

"Oh, oh God!" Jason coughed, covering his mouth and nose with his arm.

The stench! He smelled like...well, he smelled like a pig.

Those flickering dark eyes spotted Jason, widened, and his pudgy arms reached out in his direction. A sound rose out of him, starting low and winding up like a siren as his staggering waddle turned into a faltering run.

He had no tongue.

Jason back-pedalled as fast as he could and began yelling for help. He doubted anyone could hear him over the man's ragged screams. This was worse than any horror movie he'd ever seen, and he whirled to run.

Constable Wagner strode around the hotel with three officers. They stepped past Jason, caught the monstrous-looking creature with gloved hands, and just like that, the screaming stopped.

Jason stopped too. He turned around. It was like a train wreck. He couldn't not look.

The fat man stared at him, his brown eyes huge and desperate-looking, and he began to cry. Great, rolling sobs spilled forth as the officers spoke to him in soothing tones. The fat man dropped painfully to the sidewalk, still wailing, and Jason saw urine begin dribbling out of a squished-up little penis beneath the layers of fat that was his lower abdomen.

"Oh my God," Jason whispered as he staggered into the wall of the hotel. He swallowed the sudden urge to vomit. "Oh my God!"

An unmarked commercial truck roared up the street and squealed to a stop. Jason turned and watched as four people—three men and one woman—got out. The woman was easily twice the size of her male counterparts in height and build. They were all dressed in light-grey utility overalls and grey hats. With the help of the police officers, they rolled the blubbering whale of a man onto a canvas hog tarp and lifted him into the back of the vehicle. Two of the workers got in the back, two in the front, and Jason saw Constable Wagner grab the upper arm of one of the men. He said something, quick and harsh, and then they were gone in a cloud of exhaust.

Jason's mouth was open and he was sure his eyes were the size of dinner plates as he stormed up to Wagner.

"What, in the name of God, was that?!" Jason demanded as the white truck turned a corner and roared away.

"Settle down, Mr. Cameron," Wagner said in the same soothing tone Jason had heard him use when he'd spoken to the fat man. "I'm sorry you had to see that, but it's nothing to get alarmed over."

"Nothing to get alarmed over?" Jason said incredulously.

"That was Mr. Jones. He's...he's unwell. Drugs, alcohol. He lives alone out in the bush, and every now and then something like this happens. It's not the first time and it won't be the last."

"Yeah, but—"

"Look around, Mr. Cameron. Do you see anyone else getting upset?"

Jason did look around then, and no...nobody else looked concerned. The townspeople, as weird as they were, went about their evening tasks just like any other place; closing shop, heading to the hotel for supper, taking their dog for a walk…It all looked relatively normal. Then Jason thought of something and his eyes narrowed.

"Who were those people in the van?" Jason asked suspiciously.

Constable Wagner gave him a patient smile, which rankled Jason.

"They work for Schneider Pork Production. The woman, be it fortunate or not, is Jones's sister. It's easier to get him in and out of that utility truck than the back of my squad car. The boys help her out when Jones goes off his rocker."

Jason shook his head and took in a deep, cleansing breath. The Escalade would not get fixed soon enough.

"Look, don't worry about it," Constable Wagner said. "Your wife and daughter," he pointed up at the hotel and Jason saw Cindy and Mandy staring wide-eyed out the window, "will likely need some reassuring. Perhaps you can give them that."

Jason stared up at them and gave Cindy a close-lipped smile and gestured that everything was fine. She gave a hesitant smile back and nodded. Mandy walked away from the window.

"Okay," he said and tried to shake off the discomfort the whole episode had caused. He needed his run. He straightened his shoulders and gave a laugh.

"I'll take that as a sign. I'd better stick to my exercise regime, or else!"

The policeman gave Jason a look, glanced up at the window that Cindy had also vacated, and tipped his hat back with one finger.

"If you want a nice view while you're out for your run, I suggest you head straight up the hill there," Constable Wagner said, hooking his thumb in the opposite direction Jason had planned to go. "There's a trail just off 3rd Avenue. You can't miss it. Runs along the ridge behind the Plant. About ten miles, there and back. It's got a beautiful view of the valley."

"Oh," Jason said, glancing back down the main highway.

"Course, it might be a little challenging…especially since you need to be back in town before the sun sets. Pretty easy to get lost in these woods," he added, and then he shook his head. "Nah. Never mind. Stick to the highway. It's safer."

Jason felt his chest swell a little and scoffed a laugh.

"Oh that's okay," he said confidently. "I think a jog along the ridge is perfect. I can run an eight-minute mile. The sun sets at what, seven-thirty?"

"Mhmm," Constable Wagner agreed. "But—"

"Easy. I'll be back in plenty of time."

And before the man could say more, Jason took off at a brisk jog. Constable Wagner watched the trim figure bounce across the street, adjusted his gun belt, and headed to the hotel for supper.

Jason turned left on 3rd Avenue, on which were only four houses. The trail was indeed very obvious. It looked like a long black tongue lolling out of a mouth of evergreens. Jason hit the dirt trail at a run and bolted up the steeply rising incline.

***

Pebbles galloped back and forth across the hotel room floor as Mandy tossed her little rope toy in a repeated game of fetch. The little dog's brown eyes glimmered with feverous delight as she raced towards her young owner. Mandy caught the rope and jiggled it gently. The poodle *"grrrred"* her protest before Mandy said, "Drop it." Then she tossed it again.

"Mom," Mandy said, glancing up at her mother's prone figure on the bed.

"Yeah, hon?"

"Why is Dad such an asshole?"

"Mandy..." her mother said with a warning tone. But it was also a tired tone.

"Seriously," Mandy said, and she abandoned Pebbles to her toy and crawled up on the bed beside her Mom. "He is! He's so...he's so mean!"

Cindy sat up and gave her daughter a reassuring squeeze.

"Your dad is just going through a hard time. He's over forty now, and he's always had issues with his weight and self-esteem."

"Mom," Mandy said with a head shake. "He's been like this for as long as I can remember. But lately, he's gotten really mean. It's like he's obsessed with being all skinny and Mr. Healthy."

Mandy made quotation signs in the air with her fingers. She tried to make it look silly, but Cindy could see the hurt on her daughter's young face, and she felt a wave of fury. The same waves of fury she'd been feeling a lot lately. Like every time Jason opened his mouth and said something misguided and ignorant. Mandy was right; kids were far more perceptive than most adults gave them credit for. He had been acting like a jerk lately.

Cindy clenched her jaw and tried to keep her eyes from tearing up.

"You know there is absolutely nothing wrong with you, right?" she said, and her chest tightened as her daughter looked away before nodding silently.

"Mandy," she said fiercely, tipping the girl's head up, "I'm serious. You're perfectly normal. I promise. Your dad's just…"

"Being an asshole?" Mandy said with a hesitant smile.

Cindy let out a huff of a laugh and hugged her daughter close.

"Please don't swear, baby," she said. "You're still too young for that, okay?"

Mandy smiled too and Pebbles let out an impatient yip at their feet.

"Okay. Sorry for swearing, Mom."

She slid back to the floor to continue playing with the dog, and Cindy returned to staring up at the ceiling. She and Jason had been in a bad place for long enough. She could handle him picking her apart about everything, but she would not let him ruin their daughter just because he had issues with his own self-image. They were going to have *'the talk'* as soon as they got home.

The sun set behind the hilltops at 8:44 p.m. Jason was not back from his run. Mandy fell asleep shortly after nine, and Cindy sat up, the TV volume low, glancing at the door until ten o'clock. Maybe he was having a beer in the little bar downstairs. It would have been nice for him to let her know he'd made it back from his run, but what did she expect, really?

Cindy locked the door to their room, changed into her pyjamas and crawled into the other bed. *Screw him*, she thought as she pulled the soft sheets up to her chin and closed her eyes. *If her husband was too inconsiderate to at least check in, let him go sleep in his precious truck. Or on the bench outside.* It was Mills, Saskatchewan. What could possibly happen to him here? Sleep came with surprising ease, dragging Cindy under.

***

The next morning, she reported Jason missing. Constable Wagner brought in assistance from out of town and hired a local tracker. Two days after that, they found scraps of material and a bloodied running shoe just off the trail between Mills and the Plant.

"Looks like maybe a big cat got 'im," the tracker had said. "A cougar, I think."

"I'm so sorry, Mrs. Cameron," Constable Wagner said gently, hat in hand as they stood beside the repaired Escalade. "I warned him to stay out of the woods, especially with night approaching. The trail is great during the day, but a man from the city, I just wish…"

"No, no," Cindy said firmly. Her blue eyes were red-rimmed and puffy, but her cheeks were dry and her voice was steady as she spoke. "Jason could be very pig-headed. Short of arresting him, I don't think anything you said would have kept him off the trail if that's what he wanted to do."

"We'll keep looking," Constable Wagner promised. He gestured to Mandy who sat in the front seat of the vehicle, Pebbles clutched to her chest. "You two are welcome to stay on in Mills for as long as you want, free of charge."

"Thank you," Cindy replied, "but no. It will be better for Mandy if I get her home."

Constable Wagner stood on the sidewalk watching the gold-rimmed Escalade disappear down the hill before turning back to his men and the people of Mills.

"Keep up the act for the rest of the day," he said, and the dozen or so faces—the so-called police from out of town included—nodded their heads and dispersed. "She likely ain't coming back, but just in case."

DECEMBER, 2002

"Is there anything special you want to do this year?" Cindy asked as she flattened the empty cereal box and slid it into the recycle bin. "For your dad, I mean. At Christmas."

Mandy was seated in her favourite spot on the couch by the window, with Pebbles nestled securely in her lap. Snow was falling softly over the city, blanketing the jagged skyline in shades of grey and white. As always, her daughter's nose was buried in a book, and there was a short pause as Mandy slipped the bookmark into place and closed the novel before looking up at her Mom.

Mandy shrugged, sliding her fingers through Pebble's curly fur. "I don't know. I hadn't really thought about it..." Her voice trailed off and her expression grew troublesome.

Cindy hadn't said anything, but recently Mandy had gone through a growth spurt and gone were the baby-soft cheeks of adolescence. She had Cindy's high cheekbones, Jason's perfectly straight nose, and a Cupid's bow mouth that smiled more now than before...the incident. That's what they were calling it. The incident in Mills. A missing and presumed dead husband and father.

"Do *you* want to do anything special?" Mandy asked, her eyebrows climbing above the rims of her new glasses. They were sleek and kind of funky, with turquoise and gold frames.

Guilt swam through Cindy, as it always did whenever Jason came up in conversation. She felt guilty for not feeling guilty enough. How silly was that?

"I sort of feel like we should," Cindy said as she sat beside Mandy.

"Yeah," Mandy agreed.

Mandy's voice lacked conviction and Cindy gave her daughter's hand a reassuring squeeze. Pebbles poked her brown and white head up out of the fluff that was her tail and gave Cindy's hand a quick lick.

"What are you reading?" Cindy asked instead, changing the subject as she smoothed the small dog's fur.

Mandy's face lit up and her mother watched the tension leave her daughter's slim shoulders. Pebbles let out a doggy sigh.

"Oh. It's an awesome book. It's about these guys who survive a plane crash and are stuck up in the mountains for weeks. They end up cannibalizing one of their friends before they get rescued."

"Oh wow," Cindy said with a laugh. "Sounds intriguing."

Mandy giggled and rolled her eyes dramatically.

"It's human nature, Mom," she said wisely. "People do what they have to do if it ensures their survival, whether it is out in the wilderness or within their communities. Plus, look at all the religious implications. There're actually a few known groups of people in North America today that are suspect of performing ritual human sacrifice and then the group eats them. They believe it gives them special powers."

"Okay, okay—gross!" Cindy laughed. "Remind me never to get on your bad side!"

"Apparently we taste like pork," her daughter continued with a teasing nudge.

"Chicken," Cindy argued good-naturedly. "I heard it was chicken."

Mother and daughter shared another laugh and once again Cindy felt that wave of guilt rise. She wished Jason could have seen their daughter for the incredible, brilliantly minded young lady she was turning into. Mandy had always been a smart child—smarter than her and Jason put together, as far as Cindy was concerned—and since her dad had gone missing, it was like Mandy had dropped all pretences. Had he really been that detrimental to their daughter's growth? Were they truly better off without him?

More guilt weaved its way in and Cindy rose abruptly. She was seeing a therapist twice a month, had been since returning home from Mills without her husband. It was a topic she could share with George. He was an exceptional listener and seemed to be genuinely invested in hers and Mandy's well-being.

Cindy left Mandy to her novel and spent the next hour preparing supper. She went downstairs to the freezer, wincing as she did so. Her knee still bothered her. Physio had said it probably always would now. She riffled around the frost-coated shelving. She spotted a bag of Mills

Homestyle Fries and another wave of guilt washed over her. Cindy grabbed the bag and tossed it in the garbage. She headed back up with a bag of frozen vegetables instead.

AUGUST 2003

He staggered down the tree-lined highway. His breath came in wheezing gasps as his emaciated muscles strained to keep him upright and moving. He'd barely made it off the farm. His bare feet—swollen now and flattened from the considerable weight gain—were raw and bleeding, but he didn't care. He kept moving, pushing, desperate to get away. If he could just get down the highway to the main road somebody would surely save him. It was early morning; he had precious little time.

*I can run an eight-minute mile...*The thought rolled through his drug-addled brain, and he moved faster. *Once upon a time, in another life, maybe.*

Once upon a time, in another life, a lone jogger had met his unfortunate, albeit lengthy, demise after being knocked unconscious and kidnapped to a place of unspeakable horror. Many things had happened after once upon a time.

Blood dripped from the bend of his elbow—he'd torn out the IV, the "liquid diet line." That's what *they* called it. A steady, high-calorie input to encourage rapid weight gain. Sweat rolled off his pale mounds of flesh and mosquitos settled in happily to feast. He coughed, his lungs burning and the thundering of his heartbeat drowning out all other sounds.

He didn't hear the vehicle roll up behind him. Nor did he hear the chatter of the police radio or the gentle thump of the car door closing.

"Now, Mr. Cameron," said a dangerously soft voice. "What are you doing out of your pen?"

He whirled. Between the sedatives slogging through his system and his new, monumental size, he lost his balance and fell heavily to the side of the road. The early-morning sun blazed down and he raised his hand to shade his tearing eyes.

Constable Wagner stood over him, hands resting on his gun belt. He stepped between Jason and the rising sun and shook his head. Plucking his radio from his belt, he flipped the dial to the last channel and keyed the mic.

"Jana," he said informally. "This is Allan. Come in, please."

There was a two-second pause, then a burst of static, and a woman's voice said, *"Go ahead, Allan."*

"I've located the escapee. Just out on the main highway. Get the truck out here before somebody drives by."

More static.

"Oh thank God—yeah, okay. We'll be right there."

Constable Wagner slid the radio back into its holster and stared down at Jason. He shook his head again as the man began thrashing about, trying to get his considerable bulk up off the road. Spittle ran from the corners of his mouth. The hatred that blazed in the man's eyes was unmistakable, and Constable Wagner smiled down at him.

"If only your wife and little girl could see you now, eh?"

The thrashing stopped, and a guttural, wordless sound rose up. The Schneiders always removed the tongues from their exotic livestock.

"They wouldn't recognize you if you walked up and slapped them," Constable Wagner continued. "In fact, I bet they would run away in terror. Just like you did last summer from ol' Jones. Funny how things can change, eh?"

He heard the Schneider's truck approaching and turned away from the form on the ground.

"Jana," Constable Wagner said irritably when the large woman exited the vehicle. "You got to start upping the sedative on these buggers. This is the third one this year. If the wrong person comes along…"

"We can't!" Jana Schneider snapped back. "Regulations are tight, Allan. They do random inspections and test the oil. We can't have sedatives showing up in the fat we render."

Jason was crying—sobbing, actually—as he was rolled roughly onto a hog tarp and hauled up into the back of the truck. He saw the rising sun for the last time as the door rolled shut.

NOVEMBER 2003

"Please don't be mad," Mandy said as soon as Cindy walked through the door of their condo. The delicious aroma of baked French fries with their signature scent of bacon made Cindy's mouth water.

Mandy, now nearly fifteen, stood at the kitchen counter, the tray of Mills Homestyle Fries still sizzling hot on the butcher block. Mandy's face looked pained, but eager.

"I was picking up the groceries you asked me to, and I remembered what George had said about facing my fears and letting go of the past. I thought this," she pointed at the tray of French fries with her oven mitt, "was kind of like a good way of doing both. Right?"

Cindy slipped off her coat and hung it with her purse on the rack by the door. She walked into the kitchen. She picked up the cardboard box with its all-too familiar logo, her eyes roaming absently over the "made on" and "best before" dates—these were fresh, at least—and plucked a small fry from the tray. She held it up, staring at the crispy, golden brown morsel of food and felt the last few tendrils of guilt and remorse loosen from inside of her and slip away.

"Um, is this okay?" Mandy asked quietly, and Cindy looked up to see her daughter's face looking much younger than it had a few minutes ago.

Without Jason, she never would have had Mandy, and that was something Cindy would never regret. But people change and Jason had certainly changed over the years following their daughter's birth. Maybe that day in Mills had been the universe's way of allowing both Cindy and Mandy the freedom to become the kinds of people they were supposed to be.

Cindy popped the French fry into her mouth, bit down and bacon-flavoured goodness flooded her mouth.

"Cathartic," Cindy said sagely.

Mandy burst out laughing.

"Big word, Mom!"

Mother and daughter bantered happily as they set the table. Mandy had even picked up a blueberry pie for dessert. They added some chopped vegetables to their meal, knowing full well none would get touched and proceeded to devour their past.

THE BOY IN THE HOLE

"DO YOU HAVE A HOLD OF IT?" Denise yelled from the root cellar. She was halfway up the rickety ladder with a large bag of potatoes.

Her sister, Patty, was leaning over the hole in the ground, reaching for the bag.

"Yep. I got it," she replied and set the bag down with the other one while Denise retreated back into the dark hole for another.

A couple of minutes later, Denise poked her blonde head through the opening and handed up the last bag.

"We should have replaced the ladder when we did the trapdoor. It looks rotten. There's a rung near the top here that I've been avoiding because I'm afraid it'll break. I'll tell Rick to buy a new one the next time he goes to town," she said, taking the hand Patty was offering.

The root cellar was literally a hole in the ground, dug about eight feet down. The ladder led to a dirt space that housed simple shelving for boxes of pumpkins, squash, cucumbers, and carrots from that year's garden harvest. Half the floor and the back wall were buried beneath mounds of bagged potatoes. The whole underground food trove was supported by wooden beams and accessed by a trapdoor. The door used to be wood as well, but as it turned brittle, sun bleached and warping with age, Denise and Patty had worried about their boys falling through it. Their husbands, Rick and Gerald, had replaced it with a metal door. They had all, accidently, overlooked the ladder.

Denise closed the trapdoor and turned to help Patty with the potatoes. Patty bent to inspect their wares when, much to her surprise, something leaped out of the bag and went straight down the front of her loose T-shirt.

Jack and Pete were playing in the yard when they heard one of their mother's screaming bloody murder, and the other one shrieking, *"What is it?!"*

The boys ran towards the commotion just in time to see Patty ripping her shirt off over her head, yelping, "It's in my bra!"

Patty was well endowed in her bra, and Pete was used to seeing that. Jack was not. His mom was much smaller and always had been. Even when she was pregnant the *"damn things never grew,"* he'd heard her say once. So, Jack stared in awe at the giant melons being tossed around as his aunt groped her cleavage for whatever it was that was violating her. With a final frantic scoop, the intruder was tossed to freedom.

Jack and Pete saw a short green body with long slender legs and webbed feet flying through the air. They looked at each other with delight. A frog to little boys was like a piece of gold to Scrooge McDuck, and they tore after it.

Denise was doubled over, laughing, tears streaming down her cheeks and gasping for breath. Patty picked up her stretched-out t-shirt and tried to reassemble her dignity through sighs of relief and fits of giggles that sounded almost crazy.

Once the sisters had collected themselves and the potatoes, they walked back across the yard to the house. Away from the delighted squeals of their little boys as they chased and giggled, arms out-stretched, fingers splayed wide, desperately grasping at air every time the little frog evaded their grip to avoid the dreaded ice cream pail.

Much to boys' dismay, the slippery amphibian found refuge in the large chokecherry bush on the edge of the yard and disappeared.

"Aw, darn it. Come back, froggy! I have a jar of spiders for you to eat," Pete said, sounding as enticing as he could.

"You still have that?" Jack asked. "I thought your mom made you get rid of them after she almost had a *heart 'tack* and died."

"She just said I couldn't keep them in my room is all. They're in the barn by the fly trap so I can feed 'em easy."

"You're smart, Pete. I never thought of that sticky paper."

"Been a few days, we could go feed them now if you want. There's a big black one in there that spins them real good, and you can almost see its teeth."

Jack got excited at the prospect of seeing real live spider teeth and started off for the barn with Pete leading the way. Halfway there, however, Denise called them in to wash up for supper.

"But Mom, we need to feed the spiders first! *It's been days!*" Jack pleaded with slumped shoulders and upturned palms.

"Never mind about your gross bugs! Get inside and wash your hands. *Now*. We need to go to the city right after we eat, so hurry up," Denise said sternly, one hand on her hip, the other pointing behind her through the open door.

The boys jostled back towards the house as they were told.

"We can go look in on them tomorrow morning, Jack," Pete whispered.

"And maybe we can catch that frog too." Jack smiled then added, "Man, your mom's boobs are as big as my head."

"I know," Pete said through giggles. "They're so gross." They laughed as they shoved their way inside.

***

The large grain farm which had belonged to the Webb family for generations was nestled in southern Saskatchewan near the small Mennonite village of Blumenort. It had been left equally to Denise and Patty when their parents had passed, and since neither of them had any notion of moving away, they decided to add another yard to the home quarter. This let them share the farm without having to share a house, and since both were married within a year of each other, that had been a blessing.

Denise, Rick, and little Jack resided on the original homestead, which was close to a century old. The faded red hip-roofed barn dwarfed the modest three-bedroom farmhouse from across a yard that was patchy with quack grass, chickweed, and dandelions. From the front of the house Denise could watch the brilliant yellow canola fields sway in the summer breeze, hear truck tires crunching down the dusty grid road, and on a clear day, she could just make out the village on the horizon. From the back porch she could smell the wildly overgrown lilacs that crowded the yard and hear the birds singing from the chokecherry bushes. Beyond the treeline was a deep, rolling coulee that had carved the land and meandered off into the distance. There used to be a creek at the bottom of it. Patty and Denise had been quite young when the creek was diverted by a dam constructed just outside the town of Duncairn. It hadn't taken long, Denise remembered, for the creek bed to dry up and give way to fescue and porcupine grass.

Denise and Patty had grown up with many farm animals; cows, horses, chickens, and of course, a couple of dogs and half a dozen feral barn cats. But by the time they'd inherited the land, most of the livestock were gone. There were remnants of old barbwire fences still half-standing, proof that they once kept animals contained. The horses were sold before the boys had been born, and the cattle had gone to auction. The chickens got distemper and died—they'd had to burn to coop down after that—and the dogs got old while the cats wandered off. Denise and Patty had brought home a litter of kittens for the boys once, five of them, but they were all gone before the year was through. Denise had tried her best to keep them around, but she assumed the coyotes got them. After that, they didn't bother with any more animals.

The boys didn't seem bothered by the absence of a furry friend anyhow. Likely because they'd always had each other. Jack and Pete were born six months apart and had been brought up together like brothers. They had no need for daycare since both Denise and Patty were stay-at-home moms. The two boys were as thick as thieves and had been since they could walk. The family photo albums were filled with memories of the two of them having tummy time on the floor together, fighting over the same toy train, playing in mud. Her nephew Pete turned out to be a sweet kid, a little overprotective, but kind and it was very clear how much those boys loved each other.

***

Growing up was simpler on the prairies, where two little boys were free to explore, search, and discover without a lot of the worries city parents might have. Jack and Pete were five years old now and had earned a little trust from their mothers. They knew to stay away from the machinery and tractors, to keep out of the grain bins, and to stay clear of the hayloft. So, on a windy, sunny July morning, Denise didn't think twice about the boys running out to the barn together to feed their gross bugs as she sat on the back porch drinking her coffee and reading the local weather forecast on her phone.

As they raced across the yard, Denise happened to spot something hopping through the grass out of the corner of her eye. She focused on it and saw a little frog frantically trying to make its way through the tall grass away from the squealing boys. Images of Patty tearing her shirt off the day before flashed through her mind and she let out a giggle, almost choking on her coffee.

The wheels squealed against the rusty track as Pete slid the barn door open all the way to the bumper. Jack raced past him to get the sticky fly trap, grabbed an old wooden chair from one of the stalls, and stood on it to reach his prize. Pete emerged from the windowsill with a large canning jar in his hand and a sad look on his face.

"What's wrong? I got lots of flies here," Jack said reassuringly.

Pete raised the jar to eye level—or at least his eye level. He was a couple inches taller than Jack and had been for the last couple years: a fact that automatically dubbed him the boss. The jar had consisted of a couple dried leaves from the tree outside, some yellowing grass, and numerous small sticks. But the main attraction had been the four spiders Pete had collected: three little brown ones and a big black one he was sure had to be a black widow even though it didn't have the red hourglass colouring. Unfortunately, all that was left were piles of spider corpses, upside down, their eight legs curled into themselves.

"I guess I waited too long to feed them," Pete said woefully. Jack grabbed the jar and gave it a shake.

"Do you think frogs like dead spiders?" he asked.

Pete's eyes lit up. "Oh yeah," he answered. "Let's go find some! We can put them in here." Pete grabbed the jar back and dumped its contents on the barn floor. He then carefully picked out the withered spiders and put them back in the jar as bait.

The boys ran across the yard towards the chokecherry bush to see if the frog from the day before was still lingering around.

"Do you see it?" Pete asked

"Nope, nothing. Do you think frogs would live in the bush, or maybe in the tall grass?"

Jack was looking towards the sides of the yard where the oak trees grew. But when he turned around, Pete was smiling.

"What?" Jack inquired a little nervously. They usually ended up getting into trouble when Pete smiled like that.

"I know where the frogs live," he said. Jack followed Pete's gaze, which landed on the trapdoor to the root cellar.

"We're not allowed to go down there. Maybe we can ask my mom."

"No way! She'll say no, you know she will! Look, it's not a big deal. We'll go down quick, catch loads of frogs, and come back up before anyone even notices. My mom will probably thank us for getting them, cuz then they won't jump down her shirt no more. If we go down there and get them without them knowing, they won't get mad when we show them we got all the frogs. We'll be heroes. They might even make us muffins." Pete finished with a very confident nod.

Jack shuffled a bit and looked back at the house and the empty porch. His mom must have gone back in for more coffee. He did feel the knot in his stomach, the one that his mom had told him never to ignore, but he ignored it. Pete's argument just made too much sense, and he really wanted to catch a frog.

"Okay, but we gotta be quick. Let's go before my mom comes back out," Jack said, and Pete smiled from ear-to-ear.

They ran to the trapdoor and pulled it open easily

"I thought it would be heavy," Jack said

"Dad said it was *alumin-im-inum*, or something like it, and that's a light metal," Pete stated matter-of-factly and, as usual, Jack was impressed at how smart he was.

Pete hurried down the ladder first and Jack followed frantically, adrenaline coursing through their little bodies as they began rummaging through bags of potatoes.

"I got one!" Jack yelled, desperately hanging onto the squirming green frog awkwardly stuck between his little fingers. He cupped it as gently as he could and put it in the jar that Pete held open for him. With the hole-punched lid in place they went back to their hunt. The only light was from the open door above them, but the morning sun was at the perfect angle to allow the boys to search all the way to the back of the cellar. The only distraction was the shadows of the tall grass swaying in the wind.

"There's another one!" Pete blurted as he lunged forward, only to grasp a handful of dirt. As his head jerked side to side, racing to find his escapee, there came the sound of metal scraping metal, instantly followed by pitch-black. The trapdoor had shut.

"Pete? What happened?" Jack's voice sounded small and distant.

"I think the wind blew the door shut," Pete said, but the truth be told, he was guessing and a little scared. Neither boy was terribly fond of the dark. Pete could hear Jack start to panic.

"It's okay, Jacky," he said, reaching out his arm and groping the darkness. "I'll just go up the ladder and open it again." His hand found Jack's shoulder and pulled him in for a hug.

"Okay, hurry—I don't want to be down here anymore," Jack said shakily.

"You just wait right here. I'll get the door," Pete said, letting go of Jack and reaching out his arms out in the direction of the ladder. It took him longer than he thought in the pitch-black. When his foot finally found the bottom of the ladder, he told Jack he was climbing and not to worry. He carefully navigated each rung with mindful patience, but a rising unease began unsettling him with each reach up to check for the door only to find vast emptiness. The ladder was only eight feet high, but it felt like a hundred in the darkness.

Jack was huddled in the exact spot Pete had left him, squatting, hugging his knees with his eyes squeezed shut. For some reason, if he made it dark on purpose, then the unavoidable darkness wasn't as scary. He could hear Pete's movements in front of him, but suddenly he heard something behind him. Jack screeched in surprise.

"What is it?" Pete asked.

"There's something behind me!" Jack squeaked in fear.

"It's probably just a frog, Jack. There's nothing else down here. It's okay, I'm almost there," Pete said in an effort to stay calm, even though he had heard something too, and it sounded much bigger than a frog. He started climbing faster.

Jack heard Pete climbing the creaking ladder. It was taking so long he started crying a little, despite Pete's "it's okay" and "almost there." When he heard the hollow tap of steel and Pete muttering an "ouch," he presumed Pete had either smashed his fingers or his head on the trapdoor. That made Jack let out a sigh of relief, thinking there would soon be light. But the light didn't come. Instead, Jack heard the snap of wood, a short cry from Pete, and a sickening thud.

"Pete?" Jack whispered.

Silence. Pitch-black silence.

Jack started to cry.

"Pete?" he whimpered. He tightened his grip on his knees, shaking.

From out of the darkness came a sound. Jack could feel the warmth of breath on the nape of his neck. He clapped his hands over his ears, hot tears trailing down his pudgy cheeks as terror tightened its icy grip around his chest. The pounding of his heart and gulping breaths echoed beneath his trembling fingers, but it wasn't loud enough to drown out the voice he heard behind him.

"*Shhh…*"

***

"How are you doing today, young man? I heard you turned six yesterday. Did you get any special gifts?" Daniel asked. Daniel was blinking at him with pale-blue eyes through thick-rimmed glasses. His sharp bird-like features were enhanced by this excessive blinking, and sometimes Jack found it distracting.

Jack was sitting on the big brown leather couch in his counsellor's office. He was still small for his age, and the big puffy couch seemed to amplify that fact. Jack always felt like he was being swallowed by the pillows, so he sat on the edge.

Daniel didn't wait for an answer he knew he wouldn't get. "Your mom told me earlier that you're still having trouble sleeping without your light on. Is that true?" Daniel asked with raised eyebrows.

Jack gave a small shrug but continued to stare at the floor. Aside from the occasional nod, that was the extent of Jack's communication since he had started coming to therapy almost a year ago.

Jack had quit talking to adults after the accident. He didn't see the point. In fact, he didn't say much to anybody anymore, which had gotten him into trouble in kindergarten and was something he was supposed to "improve" upon for grade one in the fall.

"Well, young man, I think it's time we try something new. I'll discuss it with your mom and see what would work best for you, okay? I promise there won't be any surprises."

Jack nodded once in agreement, even though he wasn't really listening. He was thinking about his birthday presents and was excited to play with them when he got home. Daniel escorted him out to the waiting area while his mother went in to discuss treatment.

The walls weren't exactly soundproof, and Jack could hear something about "transiting," but he didn't understand it and turned his attention back to the floor. He didn't like the waiting room. The weird old lady behind the counter always smiled at him, and it made him uneasy. Her puffy white hair reminded him of a bowl of popcorn, and she wore her glasses on the end of her nose so she was always looking down at him. He never liked it when people stared.

He took his mini flashlight out of his pocket and clicked it on and off. It made him feel better, knowing he had instant light when he needed it. By the time his mother came out, the weird old popcorn lady was still staring but no longer smiling. She was clearly annoyed at the clicking noise of Jack's flashlight and was happy to see them go.

***

"I'm still surprised you agreed to Buddy," Rick said facing away from her, staring out the kitchen window.

"Well, I thought Jack could use a friend, and there's nothing better than the furry kind," Denise said as she stared at her husband's back. "Buddy's had all his shots and he's been dewormed. If there was anything on this farm that could make him sick, it can't now. And I'll admit, selfishly, I'm hoping I'll feel a better once the dog is full grown and can protect Jack. Perhaps I won't get so anxious every time he's out of sight. Besides, Daniel thought it was a good idea as well, kind of like a therapy dog."

"Right," Rick griped as he poured himself a glass of water. "Tell me again why we can't get a real fucking Therapist?"

Denise could see the worry in her husband's face. It had etched itself into the lines around his eyes and mouth, carving what looked like an extra ten years in just one. She knew he felt as useless as she and it was frustrating; but the ease at which he took these frustrations out on her was getting old.

He gripped his glass as he watched their son playing in the backyard. He watched with a look of pity. Jack had such a rough start in life and looked frail and wounded, like a baby bird that had been pushed from the nest too soon.

"Our town is too small to keep a child psychologist or a psychiatrist. Jack's on a waiting list at one of the bigger centres, but they said it would be at least a year," Denise explained, even though Rick already knew this. They'd had this conversation a thousand times.

"Well, it's almost been a year! He still sleeps with his bedroom light on and still won't talk. When is this idiot going to try something new?"

Rick's patience was paper-thin these days, and Denise wasn't sure who she was more frustrated with, her child or her husband. She sat at the table and sighed.

"Look, honey, our hands are tied. There's nothing we can do about it, and Daniel is who we have to work with at the moment. He did suggest a way to help with Jack's phobia of the dark, so I'm going to try that tonight."

Denise rubbed her temples and continued with her eyes closed.

"He'll get better Rick. We just need to be supportive and patient. Our little boy went through hell and needs time to heal. We all do."

Rick's tone softened and he let out a sigh.

"You're right, I'm sorry," he stated as he turned from the window. "I just want him to have a normal life. One without monsters and death."

He kissed her on the cheek and gave her shoulders a squeeze as he made his way to the front door. "I'm glad we got the dog. It is a good idea. I'll be in the garage if you need me."

Denise stood up from the table and peered out the kitchen window to watch her son wander out towards the coulee behind their property. He had his new *Explorer's Backpack* she had given him for his birthday, complete with a safari-style helmet and the new golden retriever puppy. The pup leaped and stumbled beside the boy, ears flapping as he tugged at the straps on Jack's backpack.

She smiled, her son's elated sense of adventure reminding her of happier times. She remembered the morning Rick had asked her to marry him as they walked out by the coulee. She remembered how excited she had felt at the prospect of a new life together and starting a family. Denise had even imagined their children. What they would look like, how many they would have…she'd known they were going to be the best parents.

She sighed as her thoughts snapped back to the present. Having a child hadn't been easy for her and Rick and there were times when Denise felt like she had already failed as a parent. She watched Jack venture out of the yard with his puppy in tow and hoped she would be proven wrong.

***

Jack walked past the place where the chokecherry bushes used to be (his mom had them dug up so she could have a clear line of sight from the kitchen window and the deck), and then he walked over a mound of solid earth where there had once been an eight-foot-deep hole in the ground. An eight-foot-deep hole that used to be covered by an aluminum trapdoor. He slowly inspected his wares. Jack's new backpack had a magnifying glass, butterfly net, compass, tweezers, binoculars, flashlight, and a clear plastic container with a hole-punched lid. But the best part, by far, was the safari hat. The moment he'd put it on, he imagined a vast dense jungle crawling with snakes that were longer than the car and spiders bigger than his head. He couldn't wait to go catch his prey.

Jack was chasing a small purple butterfly with his net when he realized how far he near he was to the coulee and how close he was to the "hole." Buddy was excitedly sniffing the ground at the entrance when Jack picked him up. He was afraid the puppy might go in. The first time his dad had taken him gopher hunting, Jack had seen this enormous hole in the side of the hill. He was sure a bear lived in it, but his dad had laughed.

"No, son," his dad had told him, "it isn't big enough for a bear. It used to be a badger hole, only about a foot or two across, but the dogs were relentless with their digging and trying to catch it that they turned it into a fair-sized den. Anyways, you stay out of there. I don't think there's anything living in there now, but you never know. Badgers are nasty and mean. One killed one of Grandma's dogs, and one could kill you too if it thinks you're a threat."

Jack could still see the house from the hole, so he wasn't breaking his mom's rule, which sort of gave him permission for a closer look. He used to imagine it led to another world, one that had tunnels made by giant worms you could ride like a subway, or a vast underground jungle that still had dinosaurs, cut off from the world above. Now he mostly thought it was too dark.

He set Buddy down behind him and took off his backpack. He carefully placed the butterfly net inside and grabbed his new flashlight. He squatted in front of the hole and peered inside. It was easily big enough for him to crawl into. The idea made him shiver a bit. As he panned his light towards the darkest part, something moved. Jack jumped back but kept the light shining inside. Whatever it was had thankfully scurried deeper into the hole instead of jumping out and biting his face off. Buddy let out a short puppy growl followed by a little yelp, then started wagging his tail. Jack supposed the pup wouldn't be much help if something did come out of the hole, but he sure was cute.

"Jack!" he heard his mom calling faintly in the distance, probably for supper, and it occurred to him that maybe whatever was living in the hole might be his friend if he gave it food. He reached into his bag once more and pulled out a chocolate chip granola bar. He unwrapped it and laid it at the mouth of the hole.

"These are my favourite," he said into the dark. He picked up Buddy, who was trying to get the treat himself, then turned and ran for home.

***

"It's okay, sweetheart," Denise whispered to Jack as she held him in her lap on the edge of his bed. She combed his light brown hair with her fingers, then grabbed a tissue from the nightstand and told him to blow. When she first mentioned that it was transition night, Jack had gone into panic mode before she had time to explain fully. So she held her weeping boy and softly sang "You Are My Sunshine" to him until he started to relax. It was what her mom had sang to her when she was little; it used to make her sad, but now it was comforting. She laughed a little on the inside when she thought how oddly fitting the song was to Jack's current fear.

"Sweetheart, I didn't mean we were going to make you sleep in the dark. I'm not trying to take your sunshine away. You just can't have the main light on anymore. Look at what I got you instead."

She sat Jack on the edge of his jungle-themed bed and reached around the doorway into the hall. What she pulled up from the floor made Jack's big brown eyes light up and he smiled wide as he wiped his tears.

"It's a dinosaur lamp!" Denise announced. "The lightbulb is inside so the whole thing glows. Do you want to plug him in?"

She pulled the T. rex out of the box and Jack reached behind his nightstand to plug it into the wall.

"Let's test it out. I'm going to turn the main light off, okay?" Denise asked.

Jack stood beside her and held her hand. She turned the light off to assess how much illumination the little dinosaur provided. Judging from the way Jack was squeezing her arm, it wasn't enough. Jack felt like a chicken for crying, but he just couldn't help it. The second it became dark, he was right back in the cellar. He shook his head to get rid of the thought and looked around the room.

"It's okay, sweetheart. I also got you these, just in case," she said as she also produced a couple of night lights. She plugged them in on opposite sides of his room, and with all of them on, there was hardly a shadow left. It wasn't much different from having his main light on and Jack was okay with it. He settled down, wiping the last of his tears away. He hugged and kissed his mother goodnight and laid in bed staring at his new lamp as Denise shut the door.

I'm taking this as a win, Denise thought to herself as she descended the stairs to join Rick on the couch. *Not a lot of difference in light, but it's a change. Change is good.*

Jack stared at the glowing T. rex with its bared teeth and splayed arms. He wished he wasn't so scared of the dark. He didn't like crying like that. At least he had been with his mom and not his dad. Jack didn't like the way his dad looked at him when he cried. It made him feel smaller than he already was. He also wished that his mom would let Buddy sleep with him. Jack had told her he might not be as scared of the dark with the dog there, but she'd said no because Buddy wasn't entirely house-trained yet. Besides, his mom had wanted Jack to be okay with sleeping in the dark by himself.

The thought made him sick to his stomach. Jack could hardly remember what it was like to not be afraid of the dark. Then he thought maybe someday, when he was bigger, he would just forget that he was afraid of the dark. Maybe he would even forget about Pete and the accident in the root cellar…

Jack shook his head and rubbed his eyes. He didn't want to think about that anymore. His eyes drifted back to the dinosaur. Even though the light came from the floor instead of the ceiling, it was softer than the main light. Jack decided he liked it better. He closed his eyes and fell asleep.

***

Nightshades

As soon as Jack was done eating breakfast the next morning, he was out the door with his safari hat and backpack, Buddy bounding happily along behind him. He was excited to see if he had made another friend with the granola bar. He hurried across the yard and out into the coulee towards the hole in the side of the hill. As he approached the mouth his heart rate sped up because he could see the granola bar was gone. He turned to share his happiness with Buddy only to see the puppy was distracted with a large grasshopper.

Jack turned his attention back to the hole and decided to be a little more cautious this time. He took his backpack off, dug around for his flashlight, and then put the pack back on in case he needed to make a quick getaway. He slowly crouched down and stared into the hole. Nothing moved. He listened intently, keeping as still as he could. He felt the sun's warmth on the back of his neck and a mild breeze across his cheeks, and he smelled the wild grass and dirt. Different scenarios had been playing through his mind all morning: playing with baby badgers, as the happy mom badger smiled lovingly at them, or a litter of bunnies that had been abandoned and which Jack would *have* to take home because if he didn't they were gonna die. He excitedly turned on his light and crept a little closer to get a better look inside.

"Don't. I don't like the light," said a small voice from inside the hole.

Jack jumped about a mile in the air and gasped as he scrambled backwards. He had expected a warning growl or a dog-like whimper, but he'd never expected the English language. His heart was pounding and his whole body was numb with adrenaline, but he didn't run; he wasn't sure if he could. Besides, regardless of the surprise voice, it held no malice, and it sounded young, like his own. Buddy came over to see what all the fuss was about and started licking Jack's face.

"I'm sorry, I didn't mean to scare you. I just wanted to thank you for the food you left. It was good," the voice said.

Buddy gave a little yip and Jack was dumbfounded. All he could muster was deep open-mouthed breaths and a wide stare. He wasn't sure what to do—he wasn't even sure if his pants were still dry.

"Are you okay? Can you talk?" the voice asked.

Jack shook his head and gathered some wits.

"Uh, um, yeah. I...I can talk," he stuttered. "Who are you? Are you stuck?"

"No, I'm not stuck," the voice giggled. "I live here."

"Huh?" Jack asked, bewildered. He wasn't entirely sure he had heard him right.

"I did have a bigger home, but it disappeared, so now I live here," the voice said a little sadly. "It's alright though, cozy."

"So what's your name?" Jack asked.

He had started to relax a little and sat up to dust himself off a bit but was still tense enough to take off running at a moment's notice. Buddy was getting curious and sniffing around the ground. Jack picked him up and held onto him just in case.

"Name? I don't have one. What's your name? Is that a dog?"

"I'm Jack. And this is my puppy, Buddy," he said. "How come you don't have a name? Didn't your mom and dad give you one?"

"No. I don't have a mom or dad," the voice said with a hint of annoyance. "Why do I need a name, anyways? It's not like I talk to anyone."

"I don't talk to anyone really either. But what do I call you if you don't have a name? Should I make one up?" Jack asked, looking around and trying to think of a good one. His eyes settled on his initials, which he had scratched into the handle of his flashlight. "My middle name is Andrew, but I always liked Andy better. We could share it, if you wanted."

After a short pause, he got a reply. "Okay, sure. Andy is as good a name as any. Does this mean you're coming back?"

Jack surprised himself when he said, "Yeah, I guess. I'll even bring another granola bar. My mom and me are going to the city today for swimming lessons and shopping. So I probably won't be able to come back 'till tomorrow."

"That's okay. I'll be here. I'm always here," Andy said reassuringly.

Jack waved goodbye to his new friend and hurried off with Buddy in his arms. But before he got too far, he needed to know something and stopped.

"Um, Andy? Do you ride giant worms down there?"

"Uh, no. Worms are tiny, Jack."

"Oh y-yeah, I knew that," Jack stammered. *Darn—that was disappointing.*

"Okay, tomorrow then!" And then he took off again.

All sorts of thoughts were running through Jack's young brain as he ran back towards the house. He had many more questions, like if Andy didn't have parents, then who gave him his rules? Told him to take a bath? Told him what to wear or took him to the doctor? At that thought Jack stopped and looked back out into the coulee towards the hole at what he now presumed was the luckiest kid ever, even without the giant worms.

***

His hair was still damp from his bath; it smelled like Dove soap with a hint of chlorine. He had his Superman pyjamas on and was sitting on the top step. His mom had already tucked him into bed but he was thirsty, and when he got to the top of the stairs he could hear his parents talking in the kitchen. Their tone made him too timid to interrupt but too curious to go back to his room, so he sat hunched over with his hands in his armpits and listened.

"I just miss them, is all I'm saying," Denise said, quickly wiping away a rogue tear. She didn't want Rick to see just how upset she still was, but it still hurt. It had been almost a year since Patty and Gerald had left the farm, shortly after the funeral. Never in a million years had Denise thought Patty would ever leave. But she did, and Denise still felt lost without her.

"What's to miss?" Rick asked with some acid in his voice. "After what she said?! I don't miss a damn thing. If they want to pretend we never existed that's fine by me."

"She was grieving her baby boy, Rick. I know that doesn't excuse what she said, but I hate that one rash thing said in anger and grief has obliterated a family and lifelong friendship. It's insane!" she remarked as Rick stood by the single-cup coffee maker waiting for his drink to brew.

Naturally, he had his back to her. They had had this same conversation a few times, and he was clearly irritated with it being brought up again. Denise didn't care, though. She needed to talk about it, over and over again if necessary. Until it either made sense to her, or time allowed her to stop caring. Until then, she'd talk to the back of his head if she had to. Rick sighed as he reached for the cream and sugar.

"Don't you miss them? The way it was?" she added.

"Honey, for crying out loud. Why do we need to talk about this again? Of course I miss them. But what do you want me to do about it? It'll never be like it was again. They're officially divorced now. Gerald called yesterday to ask for an early land payment to help with lawyer bills. That life is over, Denise. There's no point in dwelling on it."

He paused to take a sip of his coffee.

"Besides, after what Patty said to Jack, I frankly don't want her around him ever again," he said with finality.

"I just wish I'd made sure where they were. I never should have assumed they would stay in the barn. I feel like my brain betrayed me. Honestly? How the hell did I not think of the bloody root cellar?" she trailed off.

"It wasn't just you, Denise. None of us thought of it."

"For two hours? Jesus, if only Jack had called out…"

"Stop!" Rick shouted and slammed his hand on the table.

She started and looked up at him through watery eyes. He pinched the bridge of his nose as he closed his eyes and took a deep breath.

"There's no point dwelling, Denise. What's done is done. So please, just stop."

"I'm trying!" she choked out as a sob caught in her throat. She was trying to stop crying; she was tired of crying. "But I was the one watching them that morning! I watched them go into the barn to feed their bugs and I thought now's a good time to make more coffee. Then, when I peek out the window and see the barn door is still open, I just assume it's because they're still in there. Right, because five-year-olds always close the door behind them. It had been almost an hour before I finally went out there to check on them."

Nightshades

Denise could still remember the panic in her gut when she'd realized the boys were missing. "I just can't help but feel responsible."

"Hindsight is 20/20. Besides, you're not the one they blamed. Remember?"

He kneeled beside her and wrapped his arms around her.

"I miss our old life too, I get it," he said softly. "But it was no one's fault. It was an accident. It's time to let it go. We need to move past this and find some happiness. Maybe we should try to find some time for a family vacation this summer."

Denise awarded him a small smile as she wiped her tears and laid her head on his shoulder. "That sounds like a great idea. Jack could use that. We all could."

Jack might have been excited had he heard about the vacation, but once his dad shouted, he had gone back to his room and crawled back into bed, pulling the covers up to his chin. He cried himself to sleep.

***

Jack woke up the next morning feeling like the day before had been a weird dream. Or perhaps he had imagined it. So when Andy's voice said, "Where's Buddy?" Jack had been a bit surprised.

"He's at the vet with my dad getting boosters," Jack answered.

"What's a booster?"

"My mom said it's a needle that will make him better. I'm thinking it'll make him really fast, like a turbo."

Jack pulled out his collection jar to show it off.

"Oh? What's that?" Andy asked.

"My spiders."

Jack held the jar of leaves and sticks closer to the hole.

"I got a couple brown ones and a white one with long legs. They're not as big as the black one we caught last year, but they're still pretty cool."

"I like spiders. I've seen all kinds. Even saw a wolf spider once; it was pretty big. How do you keep them alive in that glass?"

"There's holes punched in the lid so they can breathe, and I feed 'em the flies from the sticky paper in the barn. They don't like being

69

out in the day so I look for new webs and lightly jiggle them to make them think they caught something. When they come out to spin their food I grab them and put 'em in the jar. Pete showed me that."

"Who's Pete?" Andy asked.

Jack didn't answer. He didn't know how. He stared at his jar and said nothing.

"Okay," Andy continued, "you don't have to say. But if you know spiders don't like being out in the day, then how come you don't look for them at night?"

This time Jack knew exactly how to answer. "I'm scared of the dark," he said plainly. Normally he would be afraid of looking like a chicken, but he felt like he could tell Andy anything.

"Why? What's wrong with the dark?"

Jack shrugged as he stared at his feet. "I just don't like it. My mom says it's like her *'cost-er-fobia.'* My ribs feel all tight and I go out of breath."

He shivered a bit as the cellar flashed through his memory. Andy was quiet for just long enough that Jack was going to ask if he was still there.

"I get it," he said finally, his voice empathetic. "I'm afraid of the light."

***

"So how are you today, Jack?" Daniel was smiling at him with his usual warmth, waiting for a reply he wouldn't get. The thing is, Jack wanted to talk to him. Daniel was a nice person. But he had gone so long without talking to adults that he felt like he'd forgotten how. Whenever he wanted to say something he would freeze, like the words had gotten stuck. His mom said once it made her sad to see him looking so guilty all the time and he supposed maybe that was the reason he couldn't talk to Daniel: guilt. So he gave his usual shrug as he stared at the floor, because that was the easiest way to answer.

"Well, it's been a couple of weeks since I last saw you and your mom says you've made some progress!"

Jack raised his eyebrows and looked at him a little surprised. He wasn't entirely sure what this progress was.

"No more bedroom light! Your mom tells me you're sleeping soundly with one night light and a dinosaur lamp."

Oh, that progress, Jack thought.

"I'm very impressed, Jack. That's a fantastic step for you. We're all very proud," Daniel said, beaming at him.

Jack, however, felt a little at odds. He wasn't sleeping soundly. He was getting up sometimes to plug in the other night light.

"I believe you're almost ready to try something new. I think it would be good to keep the ball rolling and try sitting in the dark with someone. Not alone of course, but with your mom, or even both your parents. Whatever you prefer."

The look on Jack's face must've told Daniel exactly how he was feeling about this because he got up to sit next to him on the couch and put a hand on his shoulder.

"It's okay, Jack. We won't make you do anything that would hurt you. We can wait until you're ready, but just think about how free you'll feel when you're not afraid anymore. I know it probably feels like we're tormenting you, but please believe me when I say your parents and I only want you to have the best quality of life you can have. You only get one, and to let it be ruled by fear is an incredible waste. There are so many things you would miss out on. So just think about it and give it a try, okay? Is there something happy you could think about when you're feeling scared?"

Jack thought about that. He liked it when his mom sang to him. And, of course, Buddy made him happy. So he nodded a yes to Daniel.

"That's good! Try to focus on that when you start feeling scared and it will help. It would make your mom very happy. It would make all of us happy."

Jack looked at him awhile and gave him a thoughtful nod. He wasn't exactly sure what Daniel was getting at with the "quality of life" speech, but as uncomfortable and scared as he felt at the thought of sitting in the dark, he did want to make his mom happy. And if she was with him, then maybe it might not be so bad.

The ride home was normally a relaxing twenty minutes. Jack and Denise would share a comfortable silence, staring out the window with nothing but their own thoughts to occupy them. This time, though, his mom decided to ask him something.

"So I've noticed you going out with that explorer's pack we got you for your birthday. Is it safe to assume you like your gift?"

Jack smiled at her and nodded. He did very much like that gift. It was probably his favourite ever, especially considering what he had found with it.

"What lives in the big hole in the coulee?" she asked.

Jack froze. At first, he wasn't sure he'd heard her right and then he was confused by how she had found out and a little frightened at the thought of her talking to Andy, although he wasn't sure why that would scare him.

"It's just that I can see you talking out there and you always seem to hang out in front of the hole. I just assumed you had an imaginary friend living out there."

Yeah, imaginary, Jack thought. Holy cow that scared him, and he almost let out an audible sigh. He wasn't sure why, but something told him it wouldn't be a good idea for his parents to know about Andy. He just didn't think they would be okay with him being friends with a kid that lives in a hole because he scared of the light. In fact, Jack was assuming Andy was a kid. He still hadn't actually seen him.

"It's alright, you know. I don't want you to be embarrassed or anything," she said with an earnest smile. "I'm actually very happy to see you talking and laughing. But you know, I would be even happier if you shared it with me or your dad. We would love to hear about your discoveries. I really do miss the sound of your voice."

Her tone had saddened a bit at the end. Jack had caught it instantly. He hung his head and stared at his lap while the very familiar hot coal of guilt burned in his stomach again.

"Whenever you're ready, sweetheart," she said as she reached across the seat to put her hand on his and gave it a squeeze. "I'm just reminding you that you can tell me anything and that I'll always be here if you need me. I love you, Jack," she added before placing both hands back on the wheel and drifting back into a comfortable silence.

Jack, however, was mad. He glared out the side window trying very hard not to get too worked up because he didn't want to start crying. That would only bring on more questions and another one-sided conversation he didn't feel like listening to.

* * *

"So, you look kind of, I don't know, mad. What's wrong?" Andy asked while Jack paced back and forth in front of the hole, kicking stones and scowling. Buddy didn't mind at all and was retrieving every rock Jack connected with.

"I'm just mad at my mom," Jack grumbled. He sat down cross-legged facing the hole and started ripping at the odd blade of grass.

"Oh. What did she do?" Andy asked.

"She keeps saying she'll listen, but she won't. They didn't believe me. They all said I was lying."

Jack started to cry a little and stopped to angrily wipe his tears away.

"I wasn't lying," he added in a whisper.

"About what?" Andy asked.

Jack took a deep breath and told Andy the whole story. He shuddered when he was done and wiped his nose on his sleeve. As annoyed as he was with how often he cried, it didn't compare to how much he hated a runny nose. It was super annoying that these two things were went together.

"I'm mostly just tired of feeling bad all the time," he said after a short pause. "I know it was my fault that Pete died, but it wasn't on purpose."

"I don't get it," Andy said. "I thought you said Pete fell off a ladder? How is that your fault?"

"Because my Aunt Patty said so. I don't really remember, but when they found us, they called the 911 because she said Pete was still breathing. He died on the way to the hospital."

Jack paused a moment to gather himself; his voice was getting shaky and he hated that too.

"When we got home, Auntie started yelling at me. 'Why didn't you call out? He would still be alive if you had just yelled for us! How could you just let him die like that?!' I told her there was a monster down there telling me to be quiet, and that's when everyone told me to stop lying. My mom took me to my room and stayed with me there, but I could hear my dad yelling and everyone was fighting."

Jack stopped to take a deep breath and give Andy a chance to say something. He wasn't sure what he would say, or what he even wanted to hear. It didn't matter, though, because he only got silence.

"Anyways," Jack continued, "my mom said that I shouldn't make up stories about monsters. She said Pete's death was real and monsters are not. It made me sad that my family didn't believe me, but it was a lot worse when my mom didn't. So I stopped talking to them. I stopped talking to her."

* * *

"Are you ready, sweetheart?" his mom asked in her extra gentle voice. They had talked about this since dinner—well, his mom and dad had done all the talking. Jack wanted to be brave, partly because he didn't want to be afraid anymore and partly because he knew his parents would fight if he said no.

They were sitting on the edge of his bed, Jack in his mother's lap and his dad at the light switch, closing his bedroom door. The night lights had been unplugged and his T. rex lamp was silently roaring at them without his internal glow. It was time to brave the dark.

Jack remembered what Daniel had said to him about finding his happy place. He really wanted Buddy with him, but his dad said he had to stay outside, so instead, Jack would have to think of the song. He looked at his dad and then up at his mom and gave a small nod.

I can do this, he thought as his mom smiled down at him.

"Alright, Jack, here we go."

Jack closed his eyes, clung to his mom, and heard the click of the light switch. Instantly he felt cold and alone.

"You are my sunshine…"

Despite the warmth of his room, the loving embrace, and the whispering reassurances from his mom, he was back in the cellar…

"*…my only sunshine.*"

It was as if that click did more than merely switch the light to dark; it switched time. It switched the place. Jack could smell the dirt, feel the cold in his bones. He covered his ears, which amplified his breathing, and as hard as he tried to keep calm, it was getting faster.

"*You make me happy, when skies are grey…*"

He tried his best to focus on the fact that he wasn't back in the hole, it wasn't real and he was going to be brave and not cry this time.

"*You'll never know, dear, how much I love you.*"

It was then that he felt it: the warm breath on the back of his neck. Instinctively, he sucked his in and held it.

"*Please don't take my sunshine away…Sshhh!*"

"Jack! It's okay, sweetheart! You're alright! Jack!"

His mother was yelling at him, trying to talk over his screaming. It took Jack a moment to come back and realize the light was on and he was in his bedroom.

"Honey, it's okay. You're safe. I've got you."

Jack uncovered his ears and opened his eyes, but he couldn't stop crying.

"That's it. I've had it with that asshole's stupid ideas," his dad muttered as he opened the door and half-slammed it behind him.

"It's okay, my sweet boy," his mom said, "your dad isn't mad at you. He's just worried about you. It hurts him to see you so scared, Jack. It hurts me too. We both love you very much."

Jack knew his dad loved him; he said it to him often. They both did. But that didn't change how it made him feel when his dad got so angry. He also knew his anger would be the start of another fight with his mother. Because of him. Because he couldn't be brave. Just when he thought he couldn't handle any more guilt a new thought struck him. What if his mom and dad split up like Pete's parents had?

"Well, we learned that you're not quite ready and that's okay," his mom said quietly as she wiped his cheeks with a tissue. "But you know what? You lasted longer than I hoped for and that is amazing. I don't want you to be hard on yourself or feel like you failed. You faced your fear head on! That makes you the bravest person I've ever known. I'm so proud of you, Jack."

He took a deep, quivering breath and started to relax a bit. His sobs had reduced to the occasional hiccup. He was exhausted but listening to what his mom said actually made him feel better. He *had* tried. And she had noticed.

"I believe in you, Jack," she added. "I believe that you are seeing monsters in the dark. But we are going to fight them together and we're going to win. I will never leave you alone in the dark again. I love you, son."

That struck him. That one word, "believe," was what he desperately wanted to hear. It was all he ever needed to hear. That's when Jack knew how he could show progress and keep his parents from breaking up.

"I love you too, Mom," he whispered and he hugged her so tight he could feel her silently gasp in surprise, and she fiercely hugged him back.

**

"All I'm saying is what harm can medication do? Aren't we kind of running out of options?"

He hadn't even had breakfast yet and Jack could hear his parents arguing in the kitchen the next morning. Again, he opted to stay at the top of the stairs to avoid interrupting them.

"No, we are not out of options!" his mom said sternly. "He's showing progress. He talked to me last night and I'm confident he'll talk again today. He is getting better."

"How can you say he's getting better after the way he screamed last night? For crying out loud, he was in his own bedroom, sitting in your lap with me right in front of him, and he still lost his mind!"

"He talked to—"

"I know he can talk, Denise! We've always known! He chose to stay quiet because he was pissed off at us and now he's not. Whoop-dee-doo. What I want him to get better at is not giving himself a friggin' stroke just because it's nighttime. I don't see what's wrong with trying something different. It's been a year."

"I know how long it's been. Lots of kids his age are afraid of the dark. I know not to this extent, but it's very common. He's only six years old and I'm willing to give him a lot more time to get over this than you are. No."

Jack hadn't really heard his mom talk like that before; normally it was his dad carrying all the authority in his voice.

Jack heard his dad sigh. "Look, honey, I know it isn't ideal."

"Ideal?! Our son went through something traumatic, something that would screw up a grown ma, and you're only giving him a year. We were told from the beginning it would be a long road, and I'm going the distance. No shortcuts. I am not drugging him. I refuse to turn him into an emotionless zombie just so we can feel better about ourselves."

The kitchen was quiet for a while. Jack's stomach rumbled so loud he was worried they actually heard it.

"Okay, fine. It's just not what I wanted for him, and I don't think that quack is doing enough. You want to wait? Great, let's wait. But when will it be too late?" he heard his dad say, followed by the usual back door opening and closing.

Jack gave it another moment or two before heading down the stairs to join his mom in the kitchen. He didn't want her to know that he had been listening, but he was a little scared. He didn't understand why his dad would want to drug him. He had always heard on TV that drugs were really bad.

"Good morning, sweetheart."

His mom smiled at him. He loved her smile; it was always genuine and warm.

"Good morning, Momma, can I have some breakfast?"

"Of course you can, I'll make you whatever your little heart desires. What'll it be?"

"Pancakes?" Jack asked as his mom was already pulling out the mix from the pantry. *How did she know?* he wondered. She smiled at him as she bent down to pull the frying pan out from the cupboard.

"You got it, sweetheart."

They sat in silence while his mom stirred the batter and poured the perfect dollops into the heated pan. The smell of cooking pancakes filled the kitchen and Jack's stomach growled again. But it was also pitted with worry. Jack's curiosity got the best of him, and he needed to ask her. He felt like without his dad in the room, his likelihood of getting heck for eavesdropping was low.

"Momma? How come dad wants me to be *'dicted* to drugs?"

His mom looked at him bewildered for a moment before clarity came over her and she sat down, placing a plate of steaming pancakes in front of him. He started eating before she started answering.

"You heard us, huh?" she said with a sad smile. "Your dad doesn't want you to be addicted to anything, honey. He wasn't talking about those kinds of drugs. He was referring to a medication to help you get through the night."

"Oh, well, what's wrong with that?" Jack was confused; his mom had made it sound so bad, but that sounded good.

"There's nothing really wrong with it. But it's a drug, and like all drugs there are possible side effects. Look, there are lots of people out there who need help and rely on medications for that, and that's okay. Perhaps in the future you may need to go that route. *But*, you're only six, honey. That is something we don't need to think about for years yet. Your brain is still developing, and I don't want to interfere with that. Besides, I feel like you won't ever need them. You are a very strong, sweet, and brave boy," she said as she reached out to ruffle his hair, then she placed her hand under his chin to make him look at her. "I have faith you'll beat this all on your own."

Jack smiled at her and nodded his head as he swallowed the last of his breakfast. He supposed he was a lot braver than he used to be. Last year he had to have almost every light in the house on before he could fall asleep. Now he was down to one night light. That was pretty darn good. He packed some dinosaurs in his backpack, grabbed his safari hat, waved goodbye to his mom, and took off outside.

"Buddy!" Jack called on his way to the coulee. He paused to give his furry friend a chance to come stumbling out of his little doghouse at the end of the yard, but he didn't come. "Buddy?" Jack called again, but still nothing. He walked up to the doghouse and peered inside: empty. He turned to his mom, who was watering the flowers on the back deck. "Mom, where's Buddy?"

"Probably with your dad in the garage," she said with a haphazard look around the backyard.

Jack shrugged and decided to go on without him; he was too excited to show Andy his toys.

***

"*Rawr*," Jack yelled fiercely as he crashed his plastic dinosaur through a small bushy weed. Andy was laughing.

"What is that, anyways?"

"This?" Jack asked, holding up his toy.

"Yeah, I've never seen one," Andy said.

Darn it, thought Jack. *I suppose that means there's no underground world with dinosaurs...*

"It's a T. rex dinosaur. They were a lot bigger when they were alive. Like bigger than my house. But they're extinct now."

"What does that mean? Extinct."

"It means they are all dead. For like, hundreds of years."

"Good. Whew, if they were bigger than your house, then I don't want to see a real one. They sound scary."

"How come you don't come out here and play?" Jack asked. "I have more dinosaurs."

"I can't. I don't like the light."

"Why?"

"It hurts my eyes. I can't see at all when it's bright. It scares me."

Jack supposed that made sense. He certainly understood the feeling.

"Well, Daniel says to think of a happy time when you start feeling scared and to face your fear with someone you trust. Do you have a happy thought? Because you would be with me if you wanted to try," Jack offered.

Andy was quiet for a moment.

"Tell you what. If you try first, then I promise to try after," Andy proposed.

Jack was confused though.

"What do you mean? What did you want me to try?"

"Well, you could always come in here with me. There's a lot of room, I've been working on it for a long time and I know there's nothing in here but me. You can bring Buddy and the dinosaurs."

"I don't know," Jack said sheepishly. "I tried it with my mom and dad last night and it didn't work so well."

"Well…didn't they call you a liar? They're the ones who don't believe you. Besides, do they always tell you the truth?"

Jack thought on that. It wasn't like his parents never lied to him. Like the time he had to get a flu shot and they said it would only be a pinch, but he swore the nurse stabbed his arm bone.

"I believe you," Andy added. "I've always believed you."

Jack thought about this as well. Andy *did* always believe him. Andy trusted him. How could he not trust him back? He was his best friend. He looked back at his house, at the kitchen window where his mom was probably doing dishes. He thought about their conversation that morning about the drugs. Even though she had said no to his dad, it still worried him. Jack knew how forceful his dad could be when he wanted something done, and he didn't want to be on drugs and homeless like the people he saw on the TV. He turned back to the hole and took a deep breath.

"Okay, but you promise to try after?" Jack asked.

"Of course. If you can do it, then so can I," Andy said.

Jack gathered his toys and put them in his pack. He figured that if they could both get over their fears then they could play together, maybe even have sleepovers!

"Jack!"

He looked towards the house and saw his mom waving to him.

"I gotta go," Jack said as he stood up. "I'll see you later."

"Later then," Andy replied from the shadows.

***

Damn, Buddy's not with him either, Denise thought as she watched Jack run back to the house. When he had asked her where Buddy was, she truly thought he must've been in the garage with Rick. But when she went to check, he wasn't there, and Rick hadn't seen him since the night before. So, she did some hunting. She had whistled and called for him all over the house but got no reply. It didn't look like he had been in the little doghouse, so she checked the barn, where she even searched the loft. She had noticed a couple drops of blood on the back porch while she was watering the flowers but told herself the drops could have come from any one of the wildlife that lurks around at night. After a fruitless search, she gave up and went back to the garage to talk to Rick.

"I don't want to cause a setback," she explained. "What if Buddy's gone? What if Jack reverts back into silence?"

"Well, that's a real possibility, but there's not much we can do about it. But you're jumping the gun here, I'm sure he's around here somewhere. Puppies get into all sorts of mischief. He's curious. I'm sure he'll turn up."

"Ugh, why can't we have one damn pet? Why does every cat and dog we get disappear? Do you think it's the coyotes? Geez, it's like a death sentence bringing an animal onto this yard."

"Again, Gun. Jumping. Jesus, he's been missing for what? An hour? Have you already dug his grave? Would it kill you to think positive about something for once?"

"Fine. But would you at least help me look for him then?"

She sighed and left the garage without waiting for a reply.

Now she was squatting in front of Jack on the back deck, trying to recollect where they had both last seen Buddy.

"But you said he was in the garage with Dad," Jack said.

"I know, honey, but I was wrong. I've looked everywhere for him with no luck. But I talked to your dad, and he's confident he'll turn up. He's got to be around here somewhere. You're sure you haven't seen him since before you went to bed last night?"

Jack slowly nodded, sadness spreading over his face.

"It'll be alright, honey." She gave him a quick reassuring hug, not wanting to make a big deal out it. "Don't worry, we'll find him. Go play."

Jack gave her a trusting look and hugged her before running back out to the coulee.

Jesus, Rick better be right, Denise thought as she watched him go and retreated into the house.

***

"What's that?" Jack asked as he perched himself on a large rock. He noticed some dark spots on the ground leading to the hole.

"Blood," Andy replied. "I cut my foot last night. No big deal, though."

"Oh, did it hurt?"

"Naw, barely noticed. What's wrong?" Andy asked, clearly noticing Jack's nervousness.

Jack sighed and slumped his shoulders. "We can't find Buddy. My mom's looking for him."

"It's okay, I know where he is."

Jack was caught off guard and could only manage a "huh?" in response. He had never thought to ask Andy because he had never thought of him leaving the hole.

"He's here with me."

Jack was quiet for a while. Why hadn't Andy told him that earlier? Why wouldn't Buddy come out to see him?

"Sorry, Jack. I forgot to tell you because I forgot he was here. He came out to see me early this morning, and he fell asleep. Did you want me to wake him up? *Or* maybe you could just come in and play with us."

A part of Jack was actually a little excited to see what Andy looked like—if he'd be able to see anything, that is. But another part of him felt that knot in his stomach. The one his mom told him never to ignore. This time he didn't. Jack got down on all fours and peered into the hole.

"I don't know," Jack said. "Maybe Buddy should just come out here. Can you wake him up?"

"It's okay," Andy reassured him. "It's exactly like going to a friend's house to play. Buddy is here, and I'm your friend. There's nothing to be afraid of."

Jack could hear faint yips that sounded a lot like a puppy. It had to be Buddy, but he couldn't tell if he was excited or scared. The knot was turning into a vice grip.

"What was your happy place again? Maybe you could try that. Besides, you promised," Andy added.

"It's when my m-mom sings to me. I like the s-song, 'You Are My Sunshine,'" Jack stammered. He was incredibly uneasy now and feeling a little cornered. Like he no longer had a choice. He had to get his puppy back, and he had to go into the dark to get him.

"Are you sure Buddy can't just come out?" Jack pleaded.

"Just sing your song," Andy encouraged. "Buddy is so excited to see you. We both are."

Jack swallowed and took a deep breath. He remembered what his mom had told him the night before. *I believe in you.* He decided he needed to believe in himself too if he was going to get Buddy back. So he started singing, "You are my sunshine, my only sunshine."

He crawled to the edge of the shadows.

"You make me happy, when skies are grey."

Jack firmly put one hand in front of the other, squeezed his eyes shut, and for one glorious moment thought everything was going to be alright. He could do this. It was working. Then he felt a large cold hand wrap its bony fingers around his small trembling arm. The last thing Jack heard was a loud, terrifyingly familiar *"shhh…"* as he disappeared into the black, leaving all the sunshine behind.

***

Denise had finished up the dishes while watching Jack play in the distance. She was still revelling in Jack's progression. That morning was an entire two-sided conversation, and she felt like a giant weight had been lifted from her shoulders. One of the hardest things for her had been guessing what her son was thinking for the last year. It was driving her nuts with worry, especially the times he had gotten sick. He just pointed to his problem areas and she had to try and figure out what hurt and why. It was like having a toddler again, and it had been frustrating as hell. Putting the dishes away and the drying rack back under the sink, she gave Jack one more reassuring look out the window and smiled. She thought of all the good that would come with his newfound voice; the counsellor sessions alone would be much more beneficial if Jack talked to him.

She turned to go upstairs, thinking she might as well get some laundry done while she had the time. She gathered the dirty clothes from their bedrooms and made her way to the basement. She opened the laundry room door and jumped in surprise. There, in middle of a load of towels she had left in a laundry basket, was Buddy.

"You little turkey!" she said, relieved. "We've been looking everywhere for you!"

She reached down and picked up the yawning puppy and brought him right up to her face.

"How the heck did you get in here? I know someone who's going to be happy to see you!"

As she started her climb out of the basement with a tail-wagging, face-licking Buddy, she was humming to herself. When she reached the main floor she was singing out loud, "You'll never know dear, how much I love you."

She passed the kitchen window that faced the coulee but didn't look outside. If she had, she would have seen that Jack was gone.

"Please don't take my sunshine away…"

THE RIVER

SUMMER IS ALWAYS MY FAVOURITE time of year. The hot wind plays through the sun-warmed grass, ruffling the bees and butterflies—nectar-gorged and slow—from the petals of wildflowers that spring up in unruly clumps. Cicadas whir in constant, undulating waves of sound broken only by the occasional snort of the neighbour's horses as they graze, one step at a time, across their pasture. Long tails of black, brown and grey swish back and forth across gleaming flanks and rounded bellies. Their ears flick back and forth and their eyes, like liquid pools of dark honey, are ever watchful.

No matter how many times I've tried to approach them, I never get within more than a few feet. They don't run away. They just angle their great bodies and start stepping, ripping away the grass, in the opposite direction.

"Why do you waste your time with those stupid animals?"

I whirl around and she's standing there on the other side of the pasture fence. Her hair is so blonde it's nearly white. Her skin is tanned from the sun and she has lots of freckles smattered across her face, shoulders and arms. The skirt of her blue sundress is stained from picking raspberries and her dirty feet are bare. We are opposites. My hair is black and curly and it never sits nice. I'm taller, taller than all the boys in my class, even and my feet look huge compared to hers.

"They aren't stupid," I say, twirling the dandelion I'd plucked around and around in my fingers. The milk from the stem is sticky and bitter to taste.

"Well, you'd better not get caught in here again," she says. "Last time Pa beat you within an inch of your life."

I glance back at the grazing animals. I drop the sticky dandelion and get down on my belly to crawl under the barbwire fence. When I stand up and brush the grass and dirt from my hands and knees, she's already halfway down the road. Motes of dust rise up as I run to catch her. We walk in silence for a while until we enter the cool, dark woods.

She whirls and claps her hands.

"Want to go swimming?" she says.

Her eyes are as blue as a robin's egg. Eye colour is the one thing we do share, and they sparkle with desire as she begins backing into the loamy forest.

"Please?" she begs. "It's so hot!"

I'm hesitant. I don't like swimming.

"Please!" she says again, and I sigh.

I follow her to the river. I always do.

***

Sunday morning dawns hot and clear. We get up early, get dressed and walk to town for church. I notice one of the neighbour's horses is missing. The grey one. But I don't comment on that as I follow my family into the sun. I sit between Mama and Pa on the hard, narrow wooden pew, rising and kneeling as the sermon decrees. It is stiflingly hot and I'm so thirsty. I take a bigger gulp of the sacramental wine than Father Jones feels is appropriate. It dribbles down my chin and the side of the goblet. He glares down at me from beneath thick, bushy black eyebrows and I take my place in line to walk back to my seat. The altar wafer dissolves on my tongue. Mama is glaring at me and I feel a flush creep up my cheeks. I am extra good for the remainder of church. I don't squirm an inch even as she pokes at me from the pew behind us. When it's over, Mama says she and Pa are going to the Dorsey's for lunch.

Freedom!

We take off running, darting around people as they move away from the crowded church yard. She's wearing a green dress today. The colour of Easter grass. It's her favourite one. Her feet are still bare and I wonder where she's put her shoes. Mama would be so mad if she knew her shoes were gone. I follow her out of town, along the main road, and she finally slows as we hit the dirt road leading home.

"The grey one is missing," I say when we settle into a stone-kicking walk. We aren't far from home and I want to change out of my church clothes before we continue with the day's adventures. She doesn't want to go home, so I talk about the horse to change the subject.

"What?" she snaps, looking sullen because she isn't getting her way.

"The grey horse," I say patiently. "It's missing."

"It probably jumped the fence and ran away. Stupid animals."

"*They aren't stupid!*" I snap back. I'm finally angry. "They're smarter than you!"

"They are not!"

"Are too!"

"Are not!"

I don't notice the horse and rider approaching, we're yelling so loud. But I jump a mile when he bellows over top my shouting voice, "What the hell are you yelling about?!"

Joseph Randall is older than me by about four years. He's handsome enough, I guess, as far as that goes. The girls at school seem to think so, anyway. His hair is as black as mine, but his eyes are brown and he's always laughing and making jokes. He's going to be leaving home soon, he says, to go work up north in the mines. I don't say much about that. I've heard a lot of men go work up north and never come back. Pa says if the coal mine doesn't kill 'em, the drinking will. That's why Pa won't go north to work, even though Mama says we need the money.

"What's all the commotion about, huh?" he says again as his bay horse shuffles beneath him. Joseph is quick to correct the animal—hard and sharp—and I wince as the animal's eyes flare wide, showing white around the edges. The horse stops moving and Joseph relaxes. I can tell the horse is pensive now, worried. I reach out to pet his silky soft nose. The bay jerks back with a startled snort.

"Jesus H. Christ, Gracie Haddow!" Joseph swears as he works to collect the animal again. "Don't be scaring my damn horse!"

"Sorry," I say. I look past him, looking around for her, but she's long gone. She hates Joseph. She hates all the Randall brothers, so I'm not surprised she didn't stick around. It makes me mad, though, every time she runs off and leaves me alone. She'll be waiting for me at home when I get there, impatient as ever, on our falling-down front porch.

"Where's your folks at?" he asks and I tell him, still looking up the road for her.

"Come on," he adds. "Let me give you a ride home."

I snap my head up, looking at him suspiciously. Joseph never does anyone a favour.

He laughs at my expression, rolls his eyes, and nudges the horse up beside me. He holds out a hand.

"Get on," he says, and it's more of an order than an invitation now.

I know better, but I do. I crawl up behind the saddle. I love horses and an opportunity to ride one, even if it is with Joseph Randall, is too enticing. He spurs the animal into a lope and I grab him around his skinny waist. As we flash past the trail to the river, I catch a glimpse of a green dress and white-blonde hair.

Joseph takes me straight home, but he follows me up the porch steps.

"You can't come in," I say firmly. "Pa wouldn't allow that."

"I don't need to come in," he says, tossing his hat on the steps. "I can kiss you right here."

I shove at him angrily.

"Get lost, Joseph Randall! As if I'm gonna kiss you!"

"You will!" he shouts back. "You owe me! I brought you home! Besides, who's gonna stop me? A puny thing like you?"

Despite my protest, Joseph gets a couple kisses in and a very inappropriate grope. I scream and he jerks his hands off of me. I keep screaming until he swears a blue streak, scrambles back onto his horse and trots away. He yells something back at me, but I don't hear him.

"You shouldn't have done that, Gracie," she says from behind me, and I jump and whirl. "He's gonna be mad at you now."

"Well, what should I have done?" I snap back as I push my way past her and enter the cool darkness of our little house. "Let him have his way with me?"

"No!" she snaps back. "You shouldn't have done *anything* with him! Shouldn't have gotten on that horse! Shouldn't have let him bring you home! Shouldn't have—"

I hear a horse whinny from outside, and as I look out the window, I breathe a sigh of relief. It's only Mr. Campbell, our neighbour. He owns the horses I always try to pet. I glance back, but she's gone again, probably hiding upstairs in our bedroom, like she always does. I step out onto the porch, shading my eyes from the sun.

"Afternoon, Miss Haddow," Mr. Campbell greets from astride his big sorrel mare. "Are your folks home?"

"Hello, Mr. Campbell," I respond politely. "No sir, they're having lunch at the Dorsey's."

"Your daddy didn't go hunting recently, did he? Come home with a bunch of fresh meat?"

"Uh, no sir," I say. "If he did, we haven't seen any of it."

Which was true. I couldn't remember the last time we'd had anything other than watery soup, stale bread, or leathery old jerky from last fall's deer. My mouth fairly watered at the thought of fresh venison or boar.

"Why? Is something wrong with the deer in the area?"

Mr. Campbell's eyes sweep around our yard. There isn't much to see. A couple of old plough mules, a buckboard with one wheel broke, the stone boat and a small shed for hay. Our farm is nestled up along the forest and is flanked by the river. I've caught fish in the river, but not often, and only ever in the spring when the water is cold and running.

The older man sits silently upon his horse for a moment longer, an expression on his face that I don't understand, but it makes me feel uncomfortable anyway.

"Nah," he finally says. "Tell your daddy I stopped by." And he clucks to the sorrel horse and rides away.

She's upstairs in our room, as I'd predicted, and as always, she begs me to take her swimming. And as always, I do.

***

That night when I told Mama and Pa about Mr. Campbell's visit, Pa says nothing. So I go on to talk about the horse he rode, how pretty it was—though I emphasized that I am not crawling through the fence anymore to see them—and then I say that the grey one is gone.

"And just what are you implyin'?" Pa snarls, his voice taking on a dangerous edge.

I sit back fast, eyes wide, mouth open.

"Nothing!" I say quickly.

He's on his feet so fast that his chair topples over, and Mama jumps up too.

"Ray!" she cries out as he grabs me.

"What did you tell him?" he yells, giving me such a hard shake that my teeth gnash together.

Stunned and scared, I grab at his hands, trying to pry him loose.

"Nothing!" I yelp again.

"You tell him I stole that grey nag and carved it up?!"

"No!" I cry, genuinely horrified.

"Did ya?!"

"*No!*"

"Ray!" Mama shrieks. "Stop it! She doesn't know anything! Leave her be!'"

The crack of his hand against my cheek sends me reeling. I hit the bare floor with a thud, my head spinning, and Pa looms over me. Another crack and I am out. I don't feel the rest.

* * *

The next day finds me in bed with a damp cloth on my swollen face. Mama sits beside me, shaking her head. Her eyes are red from crying, and she has a busted lip. I don't have a mirror to look in, but I can feel how swollen my face is, and the taste of old blood accompanies the rest of my aching body.

"What'd you tell Mr. Campbell, Gracie?" Mama asks quietly. I carefully shake my head as tears squeeze out of my puffy eyes.

"Nothing," I whisper, and it comes out in a mumble. I gingerly touch my lip. It is twice its normal size and damp from a trickle of blood. "Nothing, Mama. I swear."

Mama nods and tries to give me a small smile. Her hands shake as she wets the washcloth again, wrings it out, and then gently wipes at my face. She spoons something into a small cup—a white powder—and makes me drink it. It's horribly bitter, but I keep it down.

She sits on the tightly made bed along the far wall, nervously twirling her blonde hair around her fingers until Mama leaves the room. The pain in me is starting to ebb away, and I feel very tired. She walks up to the side of my bed and I think I feel her cool fingers brush mine.

"Get better soon," she whispers as my blinks grow long and heavy. "We have to go swimming!"

***

I miss a week of school after the beating. Pa won't let me go. The schoolteacher, Mr. Patterson, rode by one late afternoon to check on me and Pa met him at the end of the lane. I don't know what Pa said to him—I was in the house with Mama, making bread—but I saw Mr. Patterson look past my father at the house windows, shake his head, and ride off. He couldn't have seen me, but I felt weirdly embarrassed like he had anyway.

Mama and Pa let me miss church on Sunday too. I am fine with that. It's always such a relief when they are gone. Especially Pa and his temper. I am in such a good mood that I let her talk me into going swimming again.

She skips along ahead of me, blonde hair glinting in the hot summer sun, the path we follow dappled by foliage overhead. The air smells heady with trees, dry grass and wildflowers. She's in her blue sundress again, still stained from berry picking. I don't think the stains will ever come out now.

If you follow it far enough, the river grows wide and deep. You get to a bend in the rocks and there's a pool of water there that you can swim in without getting sucked downstream. That's where we swim. She strips, her freckled skin flashing as she leaps into the water and disappears with barely a ripple. I undress and follow, but I'm a little slower. I slip in carefully and I stay close to the shore. I'm afraid of the faster-moving waters and I don't like going in under my head. I am not a good swimmer. Not like her.

She's squealing and playing, splashing and making enough noise for the both of us. I can't help but laugh a little as I watch her. She dives in and out of the murky water, blonde hair plastered to her freckled face, blue eyes wide as she makes circles around me like a little fish.

"Watch me!" she calls as she leaps off the rocks and disappears below.

I tip my head back, letting the water glide through my dark hair, rinsing it clean.

"Holy shit, what happened to your face?!" a voice says.

I jerk upright and my heart thunders in my chest. Joseph is standing on the rocks right beside me. I hadn't heard him approach, thanks to all her yelling and laughing. I look around and scowl angrily. Of course she's hiding, leaving me alone again.

"What's it to you?" I snap back defensively as I let myself drift away from the shore and Joseph. "You need to leave."

"What?" he laughs, peeling off his shirt and tossing it down next to my clothes. "I do not. You don't own the swimming hole, Gracie."

He strips off his pants and I hurriedly look away. A second later there is a heavy splash and a wave of water makes me sputter and cough.

Joseph circles me, sending little splashes of water into to my face. He is teasing and taunting me to fight back, but I head for the shore as fast as I can.

"Don't you look at me!" I yell as I reach for the rocks to hoist myself out.

"Hang on a minute!" Joseph yells, and his hands close over my bare shoulders.

I go under with a gulping scream and my mouth and nose fill with water.

It's kind of dark underwater. My vision is murky and the rocks are a greenish-brown blob about an arm's length away. I feel the tug of the river's current against my legs, gentle but persistent. I can't see anything else, but as I kick wildly for the surface I catch a glimpse of white-gold hair floating just beyond the murky shadows. I want to reach for her, but I scrabble for the surface instead.

I break free, coughing and gasping. Terrified, I reach for the rocks again. My lungs are on fire, my eyes are burning and I cough and retch. I dip down one more time. I feel Joseph's hands on me and I lash out in a wild panic. He lets go.

Joseph is yelling something as I haul myself up and onto the rocks. I roll onto my back, knees bent, coughing and choking as I pull my clothes across my bare chest. Through my watery eyes I see him crawl out and stand over me, naked and angry.

"You know what? You are just as crazy as your goddamn sister!" Joseph shouts. "She was just as squirrelly as you are! No goddamn wonder your daddy beats you! Gotta teach you girls a lesson!"

He drops down suddenly and shoves my knees aside as he drapes himself on top of me. All the air leaves my lungs in a rush as I stare wide-eyed up at him.

"I've a mind to teach you a lesson myself," he says, and his voice is low and breathy. His skin feels cold and wet against mine—gross, he's like a dead thing—and I squeal as I try to shove him off of me.

"Just like I taught your sister," he says. One hand closes around my throat while the other pries my knees apart.

I kick and fight and I try to scream. He lets up long enough for me to take a couple of gasping breaths before squeezing my throat into silence once more. It hurts, a lot. But it's over quickly. He's breathing hard and his breath smells like Pa's after a night of hard drinking. I think *this is it, he's done, I'm free*, but instead of letting me go, Joseph crawls out from between my legs, straddles my naked torso and wraps his other hand around my throat.

I'm already exhausted from the first fight, but I give it my best again. I claw at his face and arms. I see blood run in long furrows. My lungs feel like they are going to explode and my vision is going black and spotty. Joseph shifts just a little to the left and the sun blazes down, searing into my eyes like a white flame.

***

She's waiting for me at the end of the trail where it leaves the woods and meets the road. My sister Lacey gives me a sad, almost guilty smile. She holds out her hand.

"I'm sorry," she says as I reach and accept her grasp. Her skin feels warm this time and smoothly familiar. "But it's not so bad here. It'll be way better, now that we're together again, right?"

"I guess so," I say as I glance around. Everything looks familiar, but different somehow. It's still summer and still deliciously warm outside with bees buzzing, butterflies flitting, and the cicadas humming their wave of song. But the world has a softer hue to it. When I take a deep breath, everything smells just a little cleaner, a little sharper, like after a big summer storm blows through and washes the dust off everything.

I feel different too—better, actually. I reach up and touch my face. It's not sore anymore and the swelling is gone. I feel my throat where Joseph had been squeezing. That had really hurt. But it feels good too, and so does the rest of me. I wriggle, feeling my sundress slide across my skin. I touch my hair and for once it feels soft and curly, not the wire brush I'm used to it being.

"I have some good news!" Lacey says as she tugs me away from the road home and towards the Campbell's pasture. "That grey horse you like is here!"

I look up surprised.

"Look!" my sister says and when I blink, we're inside the pasture gazing at the Campbell's horses. I feel a mild sense of disorientation, but that quickly fades to the wayside. They are grazing, as always, but the bay and the sorrel look...different. Like if I reached out and touched them, they'd fly apart and disappear, like dandelion fluff when you blow on it. Only the grey horse looks real and solid. For the first time ever, she walks up to me and lets me touch her nose.

I hold my breath in utter delight. The skin of her nose is softer than anything I have ever known. Softer than the velvet of Pastor Jones's robes, even. I run my hands up her smooth, flat cheeks and spread my arms wide to reach either side of her arched neck. I close my eyes as I hug the horse. Her coat is warm and soft and she smells like summer.

Her mane is coarse beneath my fingers. I feel the heavy *thud-thud* of her heartbeat against my tummy. I'm so happy I want to cry.

"Do you think she'll let us ride her?" I ask Lacey as I let go and face my sister again.

"Oh for sure," she says. "Horses are really smart."

I squint at her.

"You called them dumb animals just last week."

She shrugs and steps to the animal's left side.

"I lied," she says. She cups her hands for me to step in.

I do.

Lacey tosses me up and up, so high I feel like I'll fly right over the other side. But I swing my leg over the horse's broad back and settle against the hard rise of her withers. I am so excited I am shaking. Lacey crawls up behind me and wraps her arms around my waist. I grip the coarse mane with both hands and cling with my bare legs.

The horse steps out at a walk, then a quick trot, and suddenly we are galloping, racing, floating across the Campbell's pasture. She clears the fence with a foot to spare and we race away. It is so easy, riding her. Better than I'd dreamed. I feel like I could do this forever, and the horse raises her head, runs faster, as if to say that she could too. Her honey-gold eyes glimmer and her pink-pitted nostrils gulp the wind as she carries us further and further away. The river glints through the trees like a blue-hued jewel, the sun is warm on our backs, and our laughter rings like wind chimes on the heady summer air. Summer is always my favourite time of year.

IT SHOULD HAVE BEEN ME

ANGELA FELT THE TENSION in her back tighten as soon as the house came into view through the rain-splattered windshield. She drove up the cobblestone driveway and parked her SUV out of the rain in the two-car detached garage. *What a shit day,* she thought, looking at herself in the rear-view mirror.

She recounted the last few hours of work…the hushed conversations that had ended as soon as she entered the room, the odd glances her way during lunch and her boss lingering in the human resources office longer than usual.

She should have seen it coming. She knew she had missed a lot of work, but she just had not been able to get out of bed some days. She couldn't sleep when she wanted to, couldn't wake up when she needed to, and couldn't make herself care enough to do anything about it. Clinical depression had made her feel hopeless, worthless and sometimes nothing at all. Her last bout had been like that. She had stayed in bed for almost two weeks, feeling like a robot with dead batteries. She'd tried numerous medications: SSRIs, SNRIs, atypical, tryciclic… the list went on. She was currently supposed to be on—what was it again? One of the citaloprams? She couldn't remember because she had quit taking it about a month into the prescription, and that had been about a month ago.

She reached for the ignition to turn the engine off and stopped. *What if?* she thought. *What if instead of turning off the car, I just reach up and push the garage door remote?* Angela sat there a moment, her finger hovering over the button that could seal her in, seal her fate. All she had to do was push it. And wait. The idea left her feeling shockingly free. To be done with her "life" was a surprisingly calming idea.

Richard, of course, would find her. She imagined him opening the garage door, waving his hands through the exhaust smoke, choking and coughing as he rushed to the driver's side door. He would scream. He would cry. He would be alone. And she couldn't do that to him. It was her birthday in two days and that meant he had planned something nice for her. Besides, she'd made it this far, God only knew how. She supposed a couple more days were manageable.

The house was a 1,700-square-foot Dutch Colonial with white siding and black trim, its gambrel roof, dormer windows, and flared eaves giving it the barn house look Angela had always loved. The backyard featured a small pond and a quaint cobblestone walkway that led from the garage to a spacious ground-level deck surrounded by flowering shrubs. It was a beautiful place to relax—or at least it would be once they got some patio furniture.

Her stomach rumbled as she reached the front door. She realized she wanted nothing more than some good comfort food, a bottle of good wine, and a snuggle on the couch with Richard to watch a movie. She was thankful for a fireplace on days like this; it had been raining nonstop since the morning, and the cold and damp had permeated to her bones.

She raced to the top step as she dug for her house keys in her bottomless purse.

"You're not supposed to hide everything I put in you," she muttered aloud.

Just when she had the urge to dump its contents on the landing, she found the keys, only to discover the door was unlocked. She stepped in cautiously.

"Honey, you home already?" she hollered, only to be greeted with silence. She dropped her purse on the entryway table and shook off the drops of rain from her coat before hanging it up.

"Richie? Hello?" Angela yelled up the stairs, but still there was no reply. She walked down the hall towards the back of the house and entered the kitchen through a set of French doors. She set her purse down on the pearl quartz countertop, opened the fridge, took out a half-full bottle of Gewürztraminer. She was headed for the cupboard for a glass when she slid on a line of water that led from the patio door to the basement door just off the entryway.

Someone had left the patio door open. She instantly felt uneasy. What if someone had broken in and was hiding in the basement? Then it occurred to her that the neighbour's black and white cat, Riddler—named for the colouration on his back that resembled a question mark—liked to visit occasionally.

"Riddler? Here, kitty!" she squeaked out apprehensively. Since he was abnormally needy for human affection, he would come when she called. When he didn't, she quietly closed the basement door and finished her text.

"Hey, Love? When will you be home? Did you by any chance let Riddler in today? If you haven't left the city yet maybe you should grab some food. Oh, and there might be a burglar in the basement," she added before she hit "send." A mere second later there was a *ping*—the unmistakable sound of Richard's text notification—and it had clearly come from upstairs. Puzzled, she started up the stairs.

As she got close to the master bedroom, she could hear the shower running in their en suite. Stepping into the bedroom, she saw Richard's clothes on the floor beside the hamper. His phone, sitting on the nightstand, lit up with a new message. She picked it up and unlocked the screen and noticed hers wasn't the only text. There was a message from her sister, Jess. She opened the message, just as two strong arms wrapped around her waist from behind.

Richard was still soaking wet, and warm, as he kissed the side of her neck. She melted into him.

"Home early! Did you miss me?" he asked, boyishly spinning her around and giving her a long, slippery kiss. She knew she should tell him she got fired, but she was scared he would be disappointed with yet another one of her failures. He was a kind, patient and forgiving man, but everyone had a breaking point. She just wasn't sure where his was. Instead, she soaked in his warmth and smiled up at him.

"Of course I did, but at the moment I miss food more." She winked and gave his toned bottom a love tap. "Get dressed and I'll order in."

She left the bedroom and stopped short when she reached the stairs. "Did you let Riddler in?" she called back into the bedroom.

"Nope, why?"

"Hmmm, okay. Just wondering," she said.

***

An hour later, they were enjoying pizza and wine in the living room. The small fire warmed them well enough, with the occasional snapping log adding a sense of comfort. They had settled on the thriller *Shutter Island* for the evening's entertainment and cuddled under a blanket on the couch. Leonardo DiCaprio was in the middle of discovering his identity when they started groping each other under the blanket. This led to kissing which in turn led to sex: slow sensual sex that ended on the floor in front of the fireplace. Sex that Angela had mostly accepted for pleasure only, seeing as that was her only choice…

"What do you mean?" she had asked her gynaecologist. After a year of trying, she had expected a glimmer of hope.

"I'm sorry, I wish I could give you better news. It's simply impossible for you to carry a child. I'm afraid your only options are a surrogate or adoption. I can give you some information on those if you like."

Angela had stopped listening at that point. They couldn't even think about affording a surrogate. Adoption, maybe. But she had heard plenty of horror stories to go with that too. In the end, they had decided just to let fate run its course, but it wasn't long before she started feeling incomplete: a woman, but not quite whole. Gradually her small insecurities magnified. A bad hair day, usually fixed with a hair tie, became three hours of curling, hairspray and tears if it wasn't perfect. She cried more than usual, mourning the babies she would never have. Mourning the life she would never have. She didn't pay much attention to her grief until the first day she decided she wasn't going to get out of bed. It took Richard three days to talk her into seeing a doctor.

"My turn to shower," she said as she pecked him on the lips and climbed over him to head upstairs. The warm water washing away the day made her feel almost as good as the sex she and Richard had just had. By the time she was finished, Richard was upstairs. They crawled under the covers and began to snuggle. She felt a brief pang of guilt at what she had contemplated in the garage.

***

The bed was moving just enough to shake Angela awake. She could hear the soft drumming of rain on the roof, and something else. The sound of heavy breathing. She forced one gritty eye open. The first thing she noticed was that she was alone in the bed. The second thing she noticed was Richard, standing at the end of the bed, staring out the open bedroom door and breathing hard as if he had just sprinted a mile.

She shot up and out of bed.

"Richard? What's wrong?"

She touched his forearm and felt a cold sweat.

"Honey, are you okay? Are you sick?" she asked, feeling intensely anxious. But he didn't reply. Didn't even turn to look at her. She tried to see out into the hall, to align her sight with his, but she saw nothing. She was just about to turn on the light when Richard bolted from the room. She heard his footfalls racing down the hall, down the stairs, across the landing and down the basement stairs. Then, just as abruptly as he had started, he stopped. She listened for a moment, but there was no sound except the faded pattering of rain outside.

She quickly turned on the table lamp just as he let out a blood-curdling scream: not a startled or frightened scream, but one born of unimaginable pain.

The light from the lamp illuminated a pair of scissors on the vanity in the bathroom. Heart pounding, Angela grabbed them, then cautiously entered the hallway where she flipped the switch to illuminate the landing. Gripping the banister with her free hand, she made her way down the stairs. She stood in the doorway at the top of the basement stairs, straining to see down into the well of darkness at the bottom. She couldn't see Richard. She listened but couldn't detect any sound. She pawed at the wall for the light switch and felt nothing but smooth surface.

Shit, she thought. The basement was the one area that had not been fully renovated. Without a light switch at the top, she would have to make her way down the dark stairs and grope for the old pull string light at the bottom.

"Honey, are you down there?" she called one more time, her voice coming out more of a hoarse whisper than a clear call. She heard nothing in response. She gathered what little courage she had left and began to descend the steps with one hand on the wall to steady herself. By the time she reached the bottom, she was drenched in sweat. Keeping one hand on the handrail, she carefully reached up with the other, into the darkness, into the space where her muscle memory told her the pull string should be, but wasn't.

Fear gripped her tighter, and she instinctually pulled her hand back. *Get a grip, Richard needs you,* she thought and slowly, shakily, reached up again. This time she found the string and wrapped her fingers around it.

She hesitated. What if there was something or someone in the dark, waiting to strike the moment the light went on? Before she could ponder it any longer and lose all control to fear, her body took over: she pulled the string. What she saw was more shocking than the monsters she had been imagining: emptiness.

There was no intruder. No demon. No crumpled heap. Just an empty room. *Where the hell is Richard?* she thought as she finally took her hand off the rail. And that's when she noticed it: red. Her hand was red and sticky. So was her arm, and as she looked down, a slow horror rose in her belly. What she assumed was sweat making her clothes cling to her was in fact blood. She stared at it in disbelief and then started to pull at the soaked sweatshirt. Just as a scream started to well up in her throat, a hand grabbed her shoulder from behind.

Angela shrieked, spun around, and nearly fell to her knees. Richard was standing there on the stair above her, looking perplexed and a more than a little worried.

"What are you doing down here? Are you okay?" he asked.

Nightshades

She looked down at her hands and saw that see they were clean. Her clothes, her hands, her arms: there was no blood. "I followed you down here," she said, her voice shaking.

He looked at her, utterly confused. "Angela! I woke up because *you* were running downstairs. Were you having a nightmare?"

She looked down at her hands again and then back up into Richard's worry-filled eyes. "Yeah, I...g-guess..." she stammered. "I must have been."

***

Richard had a coffee ready for her on the table, eggs in the frying pan, and bread in the toaster. The aroma filled her senses, flooding her with a sense of normalcy and instinctively making her stomach growl.

"Good morning!" he said.

"Is it?"

She peered out the window. The sky was dark and grey, and it was still pouring rain.

Richard smiled at her over his shoulder as he slid the eggs expertly onto the toast.

"Sunny-side up for my sunny Angel."

He brought the plate over to her.

"What are we going to do today?" she asked. After the night before, she wanted to keep busy, and not think about what had happened. She was still feeling uneasy. She needed food but what she really wanted was to get out of the house.

"Actually, I need to work for a bit this morning," he said. "I have a Skype meeting with a potential client from Calgary so I'll just be in the office upstairs. It shouldn't take more than a couple hours though, and then we can do whatever you like."

"Okay. I'll think of something," she said.

Richard smiled at her, grabbed his coffee, and made his way to the stairs.

As she picked at her breakfast, she began mulling over the events of the previous night. She was annoyed with how scared she had gotten and very irritated with the fact that she needed to descend a pitch-black stairwell in order to turn on a light. Angela smiled as the idea came to her: finish the basement. She grabbed her phone to start a list. They had enough drywall stored in the garage to finish the walls but she wasn't sure about mud and tape. She added them to the list just in case and included sandpaper. Then she started browsing through paint colours. When she got to light fixtures, she opened an app that used pictures of the space you wanted to renovate so that you could try out various items and colours: zero imagination required. All she needed were a couple pictures.

Now that it was daylight, the two small windows in the basement allowed some light in, so when she opened the door she saw it immediately: a body at the foot of stairs; a broken, crumpled-up heap of flesh and bone that lay in unnatural angles in the soft light.

When her vision began to swim she realized she was holding her breath. She sucked in gasping breaths and tried to steady herself by grabbing the door jamb. Although it was tough to gauge the size of the body, she could tell the features were feminine and the hair colour was platinum blonde. She knew who it was.

"Richard!" she screamed. "Richard! I need you!"

Within seconds, he came racing down the stairs, panic in his eyes. He grabbed her shoulders to steady her.

"What is it? What's wrong?"

All she could do was motion to the basement. He looked past her down the stairs, then back at her.

"I don't understand?"

"I think it's my sister," she said as tears welled up in her eyes.

Richard looked genuinely confused.

Angela wiped her tears and looked back down the stairs: nothing was there.

"Honey, what's happening?" Now Richard looked worried, understandably. She was starting to worry herself.

"I thought I saw Jess down there, like she had fallen." She stared at the now-empty space at the bottom of the stairs in disbelief. She put her face in her hands and shook her head. "I feel like I'm going nuts!"

"Okay honey, I hate to ask but, do you think the new medication has something to do with this?" Richard asked apprehensively. He knew she hated talking about her meds.

"No, Richard, hallucinations were not on the list of side effects." She didn't have the courage to tell him she wasn't on them anymore—that this was all her. Jesus, maybe she had more than depression. Maybe there was something far worse wrong with her. But before she could slide into a complete meltdown, Richard intervened and tenderly squeezed her shoulders.

"You know what, you had a rough night with a pretty graphic nightmare. That's enough to really shake a girl up. Tell you what," he said, "As soon as I'm done this meeting, let's go to the Blooming Fields Winery, take a nice walk, drink some wine, and relax in the..." He looked out the window and remembered the infernal rain. "Ugh, scratch that. I'll think of something, I promise."

He kissed her forehead, and she smiled reassuringly up at him as he softly closed the basement door. "But do you think perhaps you could stay away from the basement until then?"

"Ha, ha! Okay. Fine. Go." She gave him a small dismissive wave and glanced at the time on the microwave, and even though it said 10:03 a.m., she pulled the bottle of Gewürztraminer from the fridge, poured herself a glass, and took out her phone.

She couldn't for the life of her figure out why her brain was doing this, and why it would imagine her baby sister dead. Jess wasn't her biological sister; she was her first cousin. Angela never got all the details from her mother, but from what she had gathered through eavesdropping and rumours, her uncle's girlfriend, not the type anyone would call "mom" material, had decided to relocate one morning. Thus, leaving her uncle with the baby, which in turn got left with Angela's mom.

Jess was the typical "baby" of the family and had always gotten away with murder, which Angela supposed was due to her parents feeling sorry for her. Yes, Jess was a bit of a spoiled brat and had a selfish attitude because of it, but not enough to make Angela wish her any harm. She still loved her.

A half hour later, she was knee-deep in funny cat videos and awkward comics when she heard a noise at the patio door. She turned and made eye contact with the Riddler. He looked like a half-drowned rat, but she knew he was in his glory. He was the only cat she had ever heard of that insisted on being outside in the rain.

She opened the patio door so he could come in, grabbed a dish towel from the counter, and squatted to give him a rubdown. That's when she noticed he was carrying something in his mouth.

"Ew, Riddler, what did you get?" she asked, trying to look at the thing dangling from his teeth. It was a milky oval mass about the size of a walnut shell, covered in what appeared to be thin reddish veins.

"Okay, you know what, buddy? I don't know what that is, but I would prefer it outside."

She opened the door again and said, "Scoot." Riddler took the hint and carried his fleshy prize back into the downpour.

***

Richard was waiting for her at the front door.

"Ready to go?"

She had thrown on a pair of capris and a hoodie, straightened her hair, and put a bit of makeup on: maximum effort for an afternoon date. They went to a local cafe called Jerry's Diner for greasy burgers and the infamous Mills Homestyle fries, made right there in her home province. Angela never could never quite put her finger on it, but there was something about those fries that set them apart. Likely the hint of bacon-flavour they were known for.

They decided to catch an afternoon matinee at the Roxy Theatre downtown, "Something relaxing to help digest the food," Richard had said. Kind of a catch-22 since movies always come with popcorn that you just have to eat. By the time the movie was over, Angela felt close to a food coma. They picked up a bottle of Merlot from the liquor store on the way out of the city and took the long way home, listening to music on their favourite radio station.

Oh, my life is changing everyday
In every possible way

*And oh, my dreams
It's never quite as it seems
Never quite as it seems.*

"That was 'Dreams' by The Cranberries. Tune in for all your golden oldies here on 94.1 The Raven!" the radio host chimed.

"Did he just use the words 'golden oldies?'" Angela asked. "So much for feeling young."

"Well, you are turning forty tomorrow!" Richard laughed. "You're less of a spring chicken now and a little more like an old crow. Finally catching up to me," he said, smirking sideways at her from the driver's seat.

"I can literally never catch up to you," she teased, laughing. "Time doesn't work that way. Not unless you died. So I dare you to call me 'old crow' again!"

She looked out the window and waited for a rebuttal. When he was silent, she glanced at him and, in shock, jerked back so hard she thumped her head on the window. Richard's face was swollen, misshapen, and grey. A thick tongue protruded from blackened lips. His once-beautiful eyes were milky with death.

Angela's vision began to blur and a scream welled up in her throat. She covered her face with her hands and pulled her knees up to her chest.

"Angela, try to remain calm!" she heard the DJ say.

When she removed her hands from her face, she saw headlights coming straight for the car. Then everything went black.

***

When she opened her eyes, she was looking at white tile: wet, white tile. She was on the floor in the en suite bathroom. She was cold, shivering, and as if on cue, someone draped a blanket across her shoulders. She tried to grab it but couldn't; the blanket felt slippery. Her hands—crusted in dried blood—had clear plastic bags over them, taped around the wrists. She looked down at her white capris, and they too were covered in blood. The shower curtain had been ripped down, and the showerhead was dripping as if it had just been shut off.

She followed the drips down to a body in the tub, its arm hanging over the side. Someone knelt in front of her, blocking her view. It was a young man in a uniform. She squinted when he flashed a penlight into her eyes.

"We need to get you to the hospital, Angela. Can you walk?" he asked.

She made her way out of the bathroom with the young man's assistance and started hobbling toward the bed. Her entire body ached, her back was as stiff as a board, her hips creaked and her head was fuzzy with exhaustion. Her eyes fell on the nightstand where she saw Richard's cellphone. It too was bagged. On the floor next to the bed, she saw the clothes Richard had left in front of the hamper the day before.

A short balding man with thick-rimmed glasses was taking pictures. There were people in RCMP uniforms and people in EMT uniforms.

"Was I in an accident?" she asked the young man, whom she now realized was an EMT.

"It looks like you might have been, but you'll be alright," he said as he guided her down the stairs, one hand on her forearm, the other on the small of her back, ready to catch her in case she collapsed.

"What about Richard? Where is he? He was driving..." She trailed off as they reached the landing. The door was open to the basement, and she saw an officer taking pictures at the bottom of the stairs.

"What's down there? Why are you taking photos of my basement?" she asked. She made an attempt to walk away from the young EMT, but he firmly held onto her.

"We just need to get you to the hospital for a check-up, Angela, and then the police can answer all of your questions." He shifted his grip from her forearm to her wrist, and she saw the ridiculous plastic bags again.

"Why are there bags on my hands?" she asked. "Can I take them off? My hands are dirty; can I wash them?"

"Are you allergic to any medications, Angela?" he responded, completely ignoring her questions. She shook her head. She was feeling lost, alone, and cold.

The EMT quickly closed the ambulance door, but not before she saw, with clarity, a stretcher being wheeled out by two more EMTs, and on it a black body bag. Her entire body became weak as adrenaline flooded her chest, making her numb, then making her black out.

***

"Happy birthday!"

The words rang out in unison. Richard and Jess was there for her birthday. Angela slowly opened her eyes. Richard and Jess were at the side of her bed, staring at her wide-eyed and grinning stupidly.

There was something odd about the way the two of them were behaving. Angela couldn't quite pin it down, but it was something to do with their movements. They looked like a synchronized swimming team, legs and arms moving simultaneously. It was eerie, and Angela tried to shake the feeling that she was still sleeping.

"Get dressed and come downstairs," Richard said, and then he leaned over and kissed her cheek. It was a strange sensation—cool, unfeeling.

When she reached the kitchen, Jess was holding a cake with frosting that read 'Congratulations' and Richard was holding a large box wrapped in baby shower paper.

"We couldn't afford real birthday wrapping paper?" Angela scoffed as she sat at the table.

And that's when Jess started screaming. "What did you do? Angela, what did you do?"

Angela jumped back up from her seat. Jess was staring in abject horror at her, as if she was the devil himself. She looked down at herself: blood covered her hands, her shirt, and her pants. She was holding a pair of scissors. She started absentmindedly backing out of the kitchen and towards the basement door as Jess slowly advanced on her, screaming, "*What did you do?*" over and over.

Angela couldn't think; everything was foggy, and the air felt thick. She stared at her hand holding the bloody scissors. Then she backed through the door to the basement and fell into the black abyss.

***

"So, doc? What ya got for me?" Detective Constable Martens asked Dr. Sandra Heinrichs. She hated being referred to as "doc" but lacked the energy to correct him. So she ignored it instead.

"Angela Hoffman is unfit to stand trial. She's still suffering severe psychosis and needs to be heavily medicated. I have spoken to her psychologist and her family, whom confirm she has been battling severe depression for the last two years. Her inability to bear children led to large insecurities with regards to her marriage. This, combined with the trauma she witnessed two weeks prior, led to hallucinations and an inability to distinguish between real and imaginary."

"She didn't witness trauma; she caused it," Martens scoffed, crossing his arms and leaning back in his chair.

"I was referring to the text messages, Detective Martens. I have no doubt in my mind she committed the murders. That's what caused her mind to fracture the way it has. But I also believe that had matters been handled more delicately she might not have responded the way that she did."

"Look, I realize she had a few bad years and a really bad weekend. I mean, the guy deserved a beating, sure, but what she did was over the top. I'm asking, do you agree with the report or not?"

Sandra sighed and opened the manila folder in front of her. She had read the report on the crime scene, looked at all the horrifying pictures and had gone over all the facts. Combined with her own examination of the patient, it was really the only possible explanation.

"Yes, I agree," she said without looking up, absently poking at the papers before closing the folder again.

"I guess I'll see you in court." He smiled and turned to go, not waiting for a reply.

Dr. Heinrichs picked up the folder and left the office as well. She entered the elevator, pushed the button marked "B1," and used her electronic key card to gain access to the floor. She was then buzzed through another set of electronically locked doors manned by a security guard she knew only as Frank. He smiled at her from behind his post as she walked by. She stopped at a plain white steel door marked "5A" and peered through the small window. Angela Hoffman sat in the corner of the padded room looking gaunt and exhausted. She stared with expressionless eyes, muttering to herself. Despite the irrefutable proof of what Angela had done, she still felt a little sorry for her.

Angela had come home two hours early the day she was dismissed from her job. When she arrived, she had assumed her husband was not home yet and had gone to the kitchen to pour herself a glass of wine. Then she had texted him about dinner, heard the message-received notification on his phone upstairs, and went to investigate. When she got upstairs, Richard was in the shower. She had picked up his phone and saw her own text, as well as an additional one from her sister, just minutes before.

JESS
Thanks for the sexy afternoon...always a good time. But just to reiterate, you NEED to tell her! I can't hide this anymore.

RICHARD
Look I cannot just dump this on her. Angela's fragile. I'm waiting for the right moment.

JESS
Well, your moment better happen soon. I'm starting to show. I won't lie to her about who the father is when she asks me.

RICHARD
I know, Jess, but I'm not telling her that I knocked-up her sister on her birthday.

JESS
How considerate of you. LOL. I really don't think it matters when you tell her. And she's my cousin, not my actual sister. She hates me already so not much will change for us. BUT you need to rip off the band aid.

RICHARD
Yes, I know. Maybe next week.

It was at this point, Dr. Heinrichs believed, that Angela had dropped the phone on the floor. Turned towards the bathroom and saw a pair of scissors on the vanity. She isn't sure exactly when reality started to fade, or if Angela even remembers what she did in those next few moments, but she was certain it was fuelled by pure jealous rage. Angela had stabbed her husband Richard in the neck, tearing open his jugular vein with her very first slash. He also had a shallow wound on the underside of his forearm where it looked like he had grabbed his throat just as she struck him again. After that he had quickly lost consciousness and fallen on the floor. She stabbed him four more times, in the gut, and then used the scissors to remove his testicles.

Shortly after that, Angela had heard a voice shouting from downstairs. Jess had returned. It was speculated she had perhaps forgotten a personal item—perhaps the silk scarf that she was found clutching in her hands. After retrieving the scarf, she had called up the stairs perhaps hearing the scuffle in the bathroom, only to come face to face with a blood-soaked, furious Angela. It was difficult to tell if there had been much of a struggle, but regardless, the end result was that Angela had thrown a pregnant Jess down the basement stairs. She had sustained extensive head wounds and died instantly, as had the baby she was carrying.

After that, Angela had made a haphazard attempt at cleaning up and then made her way back upstairs, where she had sat down on the bathroom floor and slipped into deep psychosis.

When the police had arrived, almost a full two days later, it was noted that the patio door had been left open a crack, and that one of Richard's testicles was laying on the landing in front of the basement door (it was speculated that Angela might have carried them downstairs and thrown them at her sister before pushing her); the other was found in the mouth of the neighbour's cat who apparently made regular visits to the Hoffman's property.

The retired officer who lived across the road had found his cat with the testicle. When he went over to investigate, he noticed the patio door open and entered the kitchen. That's when he noticed the unmistakable scent of death wafting up from the basement. He pulled his cell from the clip on his belt and called 911.

He heard water running, and as he approached the landing, he saw it trickling down the stairs from the top floor. It had pooled around the front door and was leaking out the not-so-well-sealed base. As he spoke to the dispatcher, he carefully climbed the stairs and entered the master bedroom where the carpet was the consistency of a soaked sponge.

In his twenty-five years on the force the officer had seen his fair share of dead bodies, but he found it was a different matter when you knew who you were looking at. Or at least he had guessed the milky eyes staring into nothing belonged to Richard Hoffman, his body now a bloated grey pile of sloughing skin floating in the bath water. That's when he noticed the body was completely exsanguinated, with clear stab wounds to his neck and abdomen. That's also when he noticed her: Angela. She was sitting up against the wall, looking very pale and cold and covered in dark, crusted blood. She was unable to talk to him, look at him, or acknowledge his presence in any way. According to the officer, she had only stared at the floor muttering incomprehensibly to herself.

Sandra looked at Angela a little while longer. She knew Angela hadn't been incomprehensible; she'd just needed someone to listen. Sandra had listened. She knew what she was saying at that moment without hearing her; it was the same thing she'd been saying since they found her.

"It should have been me."

WILD CHILD

WE MOVED TO SPARTAN, Alberta, a few weeks before my fourteenth birthday. My dad was RCMP and this was his third posting in as many years. It was tough moving around, and even tougher making new friends.

I met Jessica Hastings the day we arrived. Mom and I were in my new room, unpacking and getting things put away, when I heard the rattle of skateboard wheels on the cracked sidewalk outside. I stopped folding my jeans and glanced out the second-storey window of our new house. I could see a pretty girl with long dark hair slowly rolling by, looking curiously at our moving van. I stared down, flinching slightly when she stopped abruptly and looked up.

She gazed at me for a few seconds, hands on her hips, before finally yelling, "Well? Are you coming down, or what?"

Mom came to the window, and Jessica gave her a finger wave.

"Can I?" I asked hopefully. My skateboard was in the garage. I remembered seeing Dad put it in there.

"Sure," Mom said. "But only for an hour, okay? We have a lot of unpacking to do."

I was gone, bolting down the stairs two at a time.

"One hour!" Mom yelled down after me.

By the time I grabbed my skateboard out of the garage, Dad was talking to Jessica at the end of the driveway. He smiled at me and gave my shoulder a squeeze.

"Jessica is the daughter of one of our dispatchers," he said. "So you'd both better behave."

I rolled my eyes. He was teasing, sort of.

"Always do, Dad," I grumbled, feeling a blush heat my cheeks.

"Don't worry, Mr. Brown," Jessica said smoothly. "This town is too small to get into any trouble."

Dad harrumphed a laugh.

"Nice try," he said, and Jessica laughed too.

"Okay, okay," she said, "I promise. No trouble from me."

"I'll hold you to that," Dad said with a teasing grin before walking back to the garage.

Like a lot of girls our age, Jessica wore clothes to make herself look older. That day, she wore a dark red push-up bra under a black tank top that clung to her curves and emphasized how short her short-shorts were from the back. When she turned her gaze on me, I had the sudden urge to squirm. I could feel my cheeks heating again when she didn't say anything, just stared at me from the top of my curly-haired head down to my sneakered toes. Unlike Jessica, I wasn't into tight tops and short-shorts. My blonde hair was usually in a ponytail, I still liked oversized T-shirts and my shorts came to my knees.

"Sweet board," she said finally. "Is that an official Andy Jenkins Girl?"

"Um, yeah," I said with a surprised lilt in my voice. No one had ever noticed what kind of board I was using. Granted I'd never met another skater girl. And the boys either didn't care or wouldn't let me skate with them anyway.

"Nice," she said. "Mine's a Black Label John Cardiel. My brother got it for me."

The bottom of her board design was a mishmash of every kind of candy imaginable.

"Awesome," I said, and I meant it.

She stepped on her board and pushed off.

"Come on!" she called out. I followed.

It was hot for June. The air smelled like asphalt and freshly cut grass. We rolled around the neighbourhood for a while, coasted down some hills, and after I successfully jumped a few times, Jessica seemed to think I was just fine. We didn't talk much, just zoomed up and down the streets, hopping on and off curbs. She got me home in exactly one hour. Mom was in the driveway with Dad as we rolled up.

With a big, dimple-cheeked smile, Jessica introduced herself to my mom and said she hoped we could hang out again soon. Mom and Dad smiled and nodded and I said, "Sure." Jessica's dark eyes were glimmering in a way I later learned to be wary of.

We kind of became inseparable after that. Our parents met and became friends. Jessica's mom, Monica, was indeed a dispatcher at the police station, and her dad, Walter, was a long-haul trucker. Jess had an older brother, Brian, and he was nice enough too, although he was quiet. He had blonde hair and blue eyes and wasn't around much when I hung out with Jessica. She liked to tease me about crushing on him anyway. It was annoying and completely untrue.

Jessica was a year older than me and definitely the leader. She was kind of a daredevil. Whatever people warned us not to do—duh—we did it, but always at Jessica's instance. *Don't go out to Flat Rock Quarry, it's dangerous,* they said. We spent at least three days a week out there, jumping off the rocks into the aquamarine waters below. *Stay out of the West Side. It's the bad part of town,* they said. We boarded up and down McCarthy Boulevard, in the heart of the West Side. One day, we saw a squad car rolling up the street and we literally dove behind a scrub of bushes. I cut my knee and Jess skinned her elbow but we huddled there, trying to peer out and see if we recognized the police officers. Spartan was a small enough city, and since we both had parents working in the force, they'd probably know who we were. We ran about three blocks, cutting through people's yards and down back alleys until Jess deemed it safe enough for us to get back on the main streets and head home.

My knee ended up needing four stitches. Mom was unimpressed, but it wasn't the first cut I'd come home with.

"I had a daughter so I wouldn't have to deal with this kind of stuff," she said as we sat in the crowded emergency room. Jessica looked at me, I looked at her, and we burst out laughing. Mom just huffed and rolled her eyes, but I could see her hiding a smile.

***

It was in mid-July when Jess and I did our first official "bad thing." It was a scorcher of a day. The weather report had said we'd probably get a storm later, and thunderheads were already swelling on the horizon. Jess and I were planning a sleepover at her house that night so we could sneak out to the treehouse and watch the storm. We weren't terribly smart at our age, but then who is?

We were skateboarding up and down 2nd Avenue, sweating and itchy from the sun and the dust. Jess'd been acting weird all day, grouchy and snappy, and even though I asked her a couple times what was wrong, she just gave me a look and said nothing. I was on the verge of leaving her to her miserable self when she stopped and snapped her board up.

"I'm thirsty," she said. "Let's go grab a pop."

"Fine," I agreed and followed her across the street to the gas station. It was a rundown little store with only two pumps out front, but the pop and candies were cheap, so we went there often.

The boy at the counter was Foster Hickmore. He was chubby with white-blonde hair, lots of freckles and mean squinty eyes that followed me and Jess as we walked up and down the aisles.

Jessica kept glancing at him, and I saw her smile a couple of times, then look down, acting shy. I watched as a weird smirk settled over Foster's thin mouth. We were in front of the drink cooler, deciding on our choice of beverage when Jess leaned into me. "When I get to the till, I'm going to distract him. You're going to grab one of those." Her eyes dropped to the shelf of alcohol next to the pop drinks.

"What?" I squeaked, my eyes going huge. "No, Jess!"

"You have to!" she hissed back. "Your T-shirt is baggier than mine. He won't notice. I'll keep him distracted. Just walk up like normal and put your pop on the counter. I'll buy yours," she added with a sweet smile.

My heart was starting to pound and if I wasn't sweaty form the heat outside, I was definitely sweaty now with fear. If my dad ever caught me, I would be worse than dead. I was a police officer's daughter. People looked up to me. I was expected to set an example—Mom and Dad had always said so.

"No, Jess, I can't. If I get caught—"

"Do it," she hissed with a ferocity in her eyes that I found frightening. "Or I'll never talk to you again."

She turned, tugged her tank top down a little, and sauntered up to the till. She set her drink up on the counter and threw a brilliant smile at Foster.

"Hi!" she said in a perky voice I'd never heard her use before. "You're Foster, aren't you? I'm Jessica, Brian's sister."

I turned back to the drink cooler, so scared my legs were shaking. Jessica's laughter floated behind me. I glanced around. Did the gas station have cameras? Could they even afford that here? God, I hoped not.

I would be so dead if I got caught.

I opened the cooler door and immediately started to shiver, more from absolute terror than cold air. I stared at the bottles of pop, then the bottles of alcohol. I was so nervous I couldn't even read the labels. I had no idea what to grab. Jess hadn't told me! She hadn't been specific. What if I grabbed the wrong one? What if—?

"Emily!" she shouted, and I jumped a mile, glancing guiltily over my shoulder.

"Pick your drink already," she snapped and she turned back to Foster with a laugh.

I waited until his eyes were riveted on the front of Jessica's T-shirt again. I reached down, grabbed the first thing my fingers touched, shoved it down the front of my shorts, and pulled my T-shirt over it. It was ice cold against my hot skin. I grabbed a pop and let the cooler door thump close.

I turned, slouched my shoulders, and walked back up to the counter. I set my pop on the counter and it wobbled a little. My hands were shaking. I quickly dropped them to my sides.

"Wait for me outside," Jess said, giving me a little shove.

Her voice sounded muffled and far away, but I did as I was told and walked out into the blazing sun.

She came outside a minute later.

"Here," she said, shoving my skateboard at me. Then she grabbed my other arm and hustled me down the street away from the gas station.

We made it two blocks before I accepted the fact that nobody was coming after us. Then my terror washed away in a wave of fury, and I yanked my arm out of Jessica's hand. I dug the drink out of my shorts and practically threw it at her.

"Here!" I shouted. "I don't want any of it!" I was starting to cry so I threw my board down and tried to push off.

"Come on, Emily," Jess said, grabbing my shoulder. "It's not that big a deal."

I snapped my board to a halt, whirled around, and shoved her as hard as I could.

I'll never forget the look on her face as she stumbled backwards and fell. She hit the sidewalk with a smack and stared up at me through her mess of hair. Her pop drink rolled onto the road, but she hadn't dropped the bottle of alcohol. She looked crestfallen and for a few seconds, genuinely sorry. For about half a breath, I felt bad. But my anger took over again and I pointed an accusing finger at her.

"How dare you!" I hissed furiously. "I thought you were my friend! Friends don't try to get each other in trouble! Do you know what my dad would do to me if he ever found out? He'd kill me!"

Jessica's eyes narrowed as she clambered to her feet and slapped the dirt off her shorts. She gave me a haughty look as she glanced around. We were in a neighbourhood I didn't recognize.

"Oh, grow up," she snapped. "Nobody is going to find out unless you turn into a baby and start tattling."

"I'm not a baby!" I shouted back, and she looked wildly at the open windows of the nearby houses.

"Shut up!" Jess snarled. "If you're not a baby, then why are you being so crazy? So we stole one bottle. Who cares? You think our parents didn't do shit like this when they were our age?"

"I doubt it!" I snapped back, but I felt a thread of doubt curl through me. Mom had joked about Dad being a "wild child" growing up and about how his parents never thought he'd make it through the police academy's training.

Jess placed her hands on her hips and gave me a disgusted look.

"Look, I'm sorry, okay? I thought you were mature enough to handle it. Obviously, I was wrong."

With that, she whirled and stalked away. Once she crossed the street, she tossed her skateboard down, hopped on and was gone.

I left my soda on the sidewalk and skated as fast as I could home. I tossed my board outside on the step, then pounded through the kitchen and up the stairs to my room. I closed the door gently—didn't want to make Mom angry—threw myself on the bed and sobbed bitterly into my pillows.

I was angry. Angry at Jess for everything, for practically forcing me to steal booze and for threatening never to talk to me again. What kind of friend does that? I rolled over, wiping my eyes and stared up at my ceiling, vowing I'd never talk to Jessica again.

I went for a shower and was combing my hair when Mom called me down for supper. I entered the kitchen and stopped short. Jessica was sitting at our kitchen table.

"Hey!" Jess greeted sweetly. "I came to help you carry your stuff for our sleepover. Then your mom doesn't have to drive you."

"And, since your dad is working late," Mom added, "I asked her to stay for dinner."

Mom's smile wilted a little around the edges as she stared at my face.

"You okay, hon?" Mom asked and I swallowed hard.

"Yup," I said quickly as my heart began to thunder again. If I'd gotten caught... "Too much sun," I added as I slid into my seat and gulped the glass of water Mom had set out. I wiped my mouth and plastered a fake smile on my face.

"Thanks for coming to help me," I said, because that's what Mom would expect me to say, and Jessica smiled back at me, big and bright and as dimpled as ever.

I wanted to kick her in the face.

We ate supper. I put on an award-winning performance, and then Jess followed me upstairs to my room to get my stuff. As soon as my door was closed, I started to shake again. I stood at the foot of my bed, fists clenched, teeth gritted.

"Why are you here?" I demanded in an angry whisper-yell.

Jessica said nothing, gliding around my room, taking in the adolescent posters I didn't have the heart to tear down yet, my closet strewn with my boring no-name clothing, and the few ornaments and little trinkets that still meant something to me. She turned suddenly to face me, and it made me jump.

"I came to make sure you didn't shoot your mouth off and get us in trouble," she said, her eyes glimmering.

"Are you insane?!" I yelped. "I...I wouldn't! *I can't!* My dad—"

"Would kill you. Yeah, yeah. You said that already." She waved her hand dismissively.

"So what are you still angry about? Nothing happened to us. Get over it, get your stuff, and let's go to my house. If I walk down those stairs without you, your mom is going to be up here wondering what happened, and I know you'll cave. I'm leaving in three."

My mouth dropped open, but no sound came out.

Was she right? Was I being overly dramatic and turning a harmless stunt into something it didn't need to be? Jessica stepped out of my room and I heard her counting as she thumped down the stairs.

"Three, two, one..."

I stared after her and made a split-second decision. I got to the top of the stairs just as she reached the bottom.

"Jess," I said, and she turned.

I threw my sleeping bag at her and it smacked her in the face as she caught it. She lowered the blue bundle.

"Meet me in the kitchen. I need my toothbrush."

We stared at each other, and then a smile curved her lips. There was that glimmer in her eyes. Despite the knots in my stomach I smiled back and went to grab the rest of my stuff.

As planned, we snuck out to the treehouse in the middle of the night and sat knee to knee as the thunder rumbled and lightening flashed across the dark sky. We shared the fruit-flavoured cooler that was actually pretty delicious and listened to our latest favourite band. Later, we lay in our sleeping bags as the rain drummed against the roof of the tree house. I felt pleasantly sleepy and fuzzy-headed.

"Em?"

"Yeah?"

"It was kind of fun, right?"

I knew what she was talking about, and I laid there silently for a minute before finally looking over at her. I could barely make out her features.

"Actually...no," I said and burst out laughing as I rolled onto my side. "I was so scared I thought I was going to puke!"

"Seriously?"

She was laughing now too. It felt good. Like we'd made up without having to say "sorry."

"Yes! My knees were shaking so hard I could barely walk!"

"Oh my God."

We laughed. It took forever for the giggles to subside, and when they did, Jessica reached for my hand in the dark and squeezed it.

"I'm sorry you got so scared," she said. "I honestly thought you were totally up for it. You're so brave when it comes to stuff."

"No, I'm not," I said with another huff of laughter. "I'm terrified of everything."

"Liar."

"Nope, it's true."

"Mmhm."

A long clap of thunder rolled across the sky, drowning out the music, and the steady thrum of the rain overhead made my eyes droop. I wasn't going to admit it out loud, but Jessica was right. It had been *slightly* kind of fun getting away with it.

***

A week went by before we were "bad" again.

"Jess!"

I could hear the fear in my voice as we stood at Jessica's back fence and watched her elderly neighbours lock their back door, enter their one-car garage, and seconds later, back out and drive off. Jessica watched them go for about five seconds before grabbing my arm and dragging me around the fence to their yard.

"No, Jess, we can't!" I insisted, pulling back. But she had a death grip on my arm.

"Relax," Jessica snapped. "We won't wreck anything."

"What if we get caught?" I squeaked. "This is breaking and entering. We can go to jail for this!"

"Oh my God, you are *so* dramatic," Jessica laughed. "We aren't 'breaking and entering.' I know where the spare key is. We're simply going to check on their house for them. They're old. What if they left a burner on or something?"

I highly doubted they had and I stood, frozen, in the middle of their backyard.

Jess stomped back over to me and gave me a shake.

"Everyone in the neighbourhood is at work. No one will catch us. The Edwards are gone up to the lake—just like they do every weekend—and won't be back until Monday. We won't wreck anything. You won't have to steal anything. I promise."

Then she darted up to the back porch, looked around, and bent down to lift the largest flowerpot. Sure enough, there was a spare key.

We stood still in the back entrance for a few seconds, ears straining, listening for anything that indicated someone might still be in the house. My heart thudded and I was getting that cold, sweaty feeling again, just like I had at the gas station before I stole the bottle of alcohol.

"Hello?" Jessica called, and it scared me so bad I jumped and made a little "eep" sound behind the hands I'd clasped to my mouth.

The house was clean and simple and kind of smelled like old people. The kitchen was modest with oak cabinetry, white walls, and bright-pink lace curtains. The dining room and living room were combined. There was an oak table and four chairs and a matching china cabinet on one side and a small couch. There were lots of family pictures on the walls. A worn, fuzzy pink and green afghan was draped over the back of the couch.

Jessica walked right up to the china cabinet like she knew what she was doing, opened the bottom cupboard, and pulled out a bottle of alcohol.

"Ta-da!" she said triumphantly. "Vodka. This stuff is the best because it has no smell. I heard Mom say one time that you can't even tell if someone has been drinking it."

"Jess," I hissed, feeling creeped out and paranoid. "You said we wouldn't steal anything!"

"Don't be a baby," she teased. "It's no big deal. It won't taste as good as that cooler *you* stole, but it'll do."

I didn't like the emphasis she'd put on the word "you" in her sentence, like she'd had nothing to do with it. Then I remembered that very small zing of fear and exultation when we'd made it, scot-free. Yes, I'd been mad and hurt, but afterwards…

She spun the cap off and tipped the bottle to her lips. She swallowed, her face went red, and she coughed and sputtered for a second.

"Here," she said, holding the bottle out.

I grabbed it, tipped it back and took a big swallow. Fire blazed down my throat. I coughed and sputtered until my eyes watered.

Jessica was giggling as she grabbed the bottle, took another sip, and handed it back to me. It wasn't so bad the second time. We each had three sips before Jess screwed the cap on and put it back. I felt a burn in my stomach, and almost immediately I felt a little fuzzy headed.

"Come on," she said, grabbing my hand again. This time I let her pull me through the living room and down the hall. The first room was small and filled with junk: boxes, sewing supplies, clothes, and knick-knacks. We rummaged around for a few minutes, found nothing of interest, and carried on to the next bedroom. They had one of those big old beds that was tall and sank in the middle. Jessica clambered on and started jumping up and down.

A giggle burst forth even as I tried to scold her.

"Do you think they still have sex?" Jessica blurted out.

"What?" I cried as she reached down and pulled me up onto the bed. "Gross! No! I don't want to think of that."

"I bet they do," she laughed as we both started to jump. The bed squeaked noisily.

"*Oh, Grace!*" Jessica grunted in a low voice, in time with her jumping. "*Oh, Henry!*" she added in a higher voice. Then, "*Ugh! Ugh! Ugh!*" as she jumped faster and faster.

I was laughing, howling actually, as I tried not to imagine the two elderly people going at it in the squeaky old bed.

I fell and Jessica collapsed beside me. We laughed uproariously, clutching our stomachs atop the rumpled bedspread.

"I bet they do it every night."

"No way," I said with a laugh. "Maybe every second or third night. They're old."

"How about your folks? You ever catch them?"

"Oh, double gross, Jess. No, I've never caught them."

She looked at me skeptically.

"Okay, okay," I said, smothering a laugh as my head spun a little. "I've never caught them, but I have heard them a few times. So gross!"

"I bet your dad rocks in bed."

I sat up fast.

"Why would you say that?" I yelped.

"Look at your mom," Jess said, giving me a shove. "She's gorgeous, and your dad is a hottie. Plus, she always looks happy and your dad's always whistling. I bet she rides him like a rodeo bronc."

"Aaargghh!" I cried, covering my ears and kicking at Jessica in mock horror. "Stop! Stop talking about my parents that way."

We laughed some more, then Jess slid of the bed and started to straighten the cover. I got up and helped her.

"Well?" I finally chirped. "Spill it! What about your parents?"

Jessica's face darkened and all the fun leached out of the room.

"Oh, they do it all right," she said bitterly. "Just not each other, unless they're hammered."

I sucked in a breath to apologize. Though for what, I did not know.

"Mom screws around all the time. She always has. She's usually doing one of the young cops when she works nights. And I'm pretty sure my dad knows, which is why he's always gone. He's got a string of ladies on the road, waiting for him at every truck stop, I bet."

"Whoa," I said quietly. "That's harsh. Why do you say that?"

"Because it's true," Jessica snapped as she punched a pillow to fluff it back into shape. "Mom walks to work, then at four in the morning when her shift is over, someone has to drive her home. The walls aren't exactly soundproof and I'm a light sleeper."

She hesitated, her dark eyes full of an emotion I didn't have time to discern.

"Last year, they were talking divorce. Fighting about it one night, actually. I heard everything. It was really bad. And then..."

Another hesitation, and I saw her swallow hard.

". . . And then they didn't. They just go on pretending they have a happy marriage. It's such bullshit. And they are so stupid if they think me and Brian don't know, or that other people in town don't know."

"Uh, I, um..."

Jessica waved her hands at me.

"Never mind!" she said with forced cheerfulness. "That's old news, anyways. Let's keep exploring. Mr. Edwards used to be in the army. I bet he has all kinds of cool war stuff."

We headed downstairs and into the den. It was dark, but cozy. An electric fireplace sat in one corner and bookshelves lined nearly every wall. They were packed full of musty old hardcovers, many of them titled in a language I couldn't understand. They looked really old. We did find some old war artifacts behind a glass case. Pictures of whom I assumed was a much younger Mr. Edwards dressed in fatigues and encircled by young men like him, carrying rifles and surrounded by army stuff like tanks and vehicles and weaponry. I couldn't name half of the things I saw.

"Holy crap. Look!" Jess said in a hushed and urgent voice.

I turned. She was kneeling beside one of the bookcases. There were old war medals on the floor beside her and a narrow, wooden box lay open next to her knees. She held up the object she'd found inside.

"Jess!" I squealed. "Put it back!"

It was a gun. It had a polished wood grain handle and the long barrel gleamed dully.

"This thing looks ancient," she said as she flipped it one way, then the other.

"Put it back," I begged. "Please. It might be loaded."

"Relax," she said, drawling the word out. "I know how to handle a gun."

"Oh really?" I snapped, feeling a bit of anger now.

"Yeah," she said as she casually aimed the gun one-handed at the back wall. "Me and my brother used to go out and shoot cans and stuff."

"With a handgun?" I challenged.

She gave me a look, rolled her eyes, and set the gun back in its little box. She replaced the medals and stuff on top and slid everything back onto the shelf.

"Happy now?" she snapped as she rose to her feet.

I glared back at her.

We didn't find much else except a box of Pizza Pops in the freezer downstairs. We took them upstairs, wrapped them in paper towels and nuked them in the microwave. They were delicious. We drank more vodka. My head was spinning now, and I felt queasy. Jessica stood up. She gave me a sheepish grin as she patted her pockets like she was searching for something.

"I think I dropped my lip balm downstairs," Jess said. "I'll go grab it. Then we should get out of here. It's almost three."

I carefully gathered up our garbage from the Pizza Pops as Jessica thumped back downstairs. A few seconds later she came back up and said, "Ta-da!" as she presented the tube of cherry-flavoured lip balm. "Let's go."

We snuck out the back door, pulling it shut behind us. Jess tipped the pot over and shoved the key back underneath. She straightened just as a car door slammed nearby.

She jumped, then ducked, hauling me down with her.

I fell beside her, bruising my hip. My stomach lurched, my head spun, and I tried not to make a sound.

"Ssh!" Jess hissed. "It's my brother."

I froze, curling into myself as small as I could and prayed he wouldn't look over the fence. I could see the top half of his face as he strode towards the back door of Jessica's house. He went inside.

Jessica grabbed me and we raced across the Edwards' yard and out into the alley. We stood there for a couple seconds, breathless, and then we burst out laughing, howling and dancing around until Brian cleared his throat and scared the crap out of us.

"What are you two idiots up to?" he demanded as we whirled.

"The only idiot I see here is you," Jessica replied tartly. She gave her brother a cheeky smile, grabbed my hand, and dragged me past him. I gave him a shrug and an impish grin, to which he rolled his blue eyes again. When he didn't follow, Jess turned back.

"Where are you going?" she asked her brother as he pulled a set of keys out of his pocket. I spotted the bike helmet he was holding.

"If Mom asks, I'm going to John's for the weekend," Brian replied.

"Are you?" Jessica asked. "Actually going to John's, I mean."

He stared at her for a heartbeat, then blew her a kiss and said, "Love you, little sister. I'll be home Sunday night. No worries."

We watched as her brother strapped the helmet onto his head and crawled onto a black motorcycle. It started on the second try, and then he was gone without a backward glance. Jessica looked worried, but then she saw me watching her and shrugged.

"He's got a girlfriend up in Taber," she said as if it was no big deal.

I had no idea where Taber was, but I nodded.

***

Monday night at supper Dad said something that nearly stopped my heart.

"So, did Jessica tell you about the break-in at her neighbour's this weekend?"

I had a mouthful of mashed potatoes. I chewed, swallowed. The potatoes felt like sand sliding down my suddenly tight throat.

"Um, nope," I mumbled, reaching for my water. My heart began thudding and I felt sweat break out in my armpits.

"What happened?" Mom asked as she cut into her pork chop.

"Not much, actually," Dad replied. "The neighbours are pretty elderly. They went away for the weekend, and when they got home, they found their back door open."

My heart thundered harder. We'd closed the door. We'd locked it, hadn't we? I couldn't remember. The vodka had made my head feel fuzzy. The Pizza Pops had made me feel nauseated. I could not remember if Jessica had locked the door. She'd put the key back, hadn't she?

"Oh no!" Mom said. "Was anything stolen?"

"Doesn't look like it," Dad replied, adding some salt to his potatoes. Mom plucked it out of his hand and they shared a look before Dad continued speaking.

"We went through the house with them. It seems like maybe a couple kids broke in, drank a bit of their booze and ate some food." He chuckled, and I stared at him, not even able to blink. "And maybe had a romp in the old-timers' bed. The sheets were a little ruffled."

As Dad snorted with laughter and Mom scolded him for my sake, I felt a heated wash of relief scald over me. It made my ears ring and the tips of my fingers and toes tingle.

"Hon?" I heard Mom say as she reached out and touched my hand.

I jerked and looked at them both.

"Sorry," I said. And then the lie fell smoothly from my mouth. "It just sounds scary! I mean, they live right next to Jessica, and with her mom always working and her dad gone all the time, what if that had been their house?"

"It was nothing, kiddo," Dad said with a wave of his fork. "They probably forgot to lock their door, is all. An eyewitness from across the street said she saw a young man on a motorcycle leaving the area that afternoon. It's possible that—"

"It wasn't him," I interrupted.

Dad's careful gaze turned to me and I felt my heartbeat ratchet up again.

"Who wasn't him?"

Oh God...what had I just done? I licked my lips, swallowed, and then took a casual stab at my peas, which rolled everywhere.

"Me and Jess were at her place on Saturday. Her brother Brian was leaving. Jessica said he has a girlfriend in Taber, wherever that is. Um, and he has a motorcycle. So, it couldn't have been him. He came out of the house...Jessica's house, I mean."

"What time was this at?" Dad asked.

I shrugged as my fingers and toes began tingling again. My chest felt tight.

"I'm not sure," I lied again. "Sometime in the afternoon. It was hot out. We were in the backyard."

"The Edwards left for the lake Saturday afternoon," Dad said, his eyes never leaving mine. "Did you girls see them leave?"

Blood rushed between my ears: *thud, thud, thud.*

"No."

"But you saw Brian leaving his house?"

"Yes."

"Dan," Mom broke in. "You sound like you're interrogating our daughter."

Dad stared at me for another second before laughing and reaching for his beer.

"You're right, it does. Sorry, kiddo," he said, smiling at me. "Sometimes your old dad has trouble hanging up his badge."

I don't know how, but I managed to finish my supper. Dad didn't ask me any more questions. I helped Mom clean up, as usual, then headed upstairs to my room. Mom and Dad curled up on the couch to watch TV. I lay awake until I heard them go to bed. Then I lay awake for a long time after that, feeling sick and scared.

It didn't feel fun this time. Someone had seen Brian leaving the area. *Someone could have seen me and Jessica!* It was nearly one in the morning before exhaustion took over and I slept.

***

Dad had some time off coming up and he wanted to go visit his parents. Mom and I were going with him. My birthday was in four days so I asked if we could take Jessica, but Mom figured we needed a break from each other. No amount of begging was going to change her mind. Besides, Jessica's Dad was coming home, she said. They needed to spend some time together as a family too. Dad said nothing other than ordering me not to argue with my mother.

Jessica acted like it was no big deal when I told her I'd be gone for a week. She didn't seem to care about my birthday either. That really ticked me off and hurt my feelings. I tried not to let it show.

"Mom says your dad is gonna be home," I said, and she looked away with a shrug.

"Yup. Super fun," she said dryly. "Gimme a call when you get home."

Then she hopped on her board and took off. I watched her roll up the street. Mom and Dad called for me to hurry up. I hesitated, then took off into the backyard. I ducked into the garden shed, grabbed the spare key we had hidden in there, and looked around for a new spot. I picked a rock in mom's flower bed, hoped it didn't rain while we were away, and stuck the key under it. Then I darted back around to the front of the house and hopped in the car.

"You good?" Dad asked and I nodded.

"Yup," I said, and he glanced at Mom.

Mom shrugged and Dad slid his sunglasses on. I stared dutifully out the window as we backed out of our driveway and drove away. We passed Jessica. She had stopped and was watching our car as it drove by. I was hurt and angry at her and I looked down, pretending to be busy with something in my lap. I don't know why, but at that moment I had the ridiculous urge to cry, beg my dad to stop the truck so I could go back and say goodbye. I felt like I was never going to see her again.

***

We had an awesome week at Grandma and Grandpa's farm. I spent my days horseback riding. Grandpa had two quiet old Belgians that carried me around their pasture. I helped Grandma and Mom in the garden, and we spent my birthday fishing at a nearby lake. I caught two jackfish and a huge lake trout. Mom took pictures while I squealed at the flapping fish on the end of my bowed rod. That night we had cake and ice cream and I opened my presents at the kitchen table. I got a beautiful blue crocheted afghan from Grandma, a John Deere hat that matched Grandpa's (of course), and from my parents, a gorgeous white-gold necklace with a brilliant, round peridot.

"Do you remember the history behind your birthstone?" Mom asked, and I smiled.

"A little. Remind me," I said.

"It's associated with prosperity and good fortune," Mom said as she fastened it around my neck. I smiled happily as I fingered the cool gemstone against my throat.

"It's also known as the 'evening emerald' because of how sparkly it is. Royalty felt it was pretty enough to be worn at any time of the day. It is believed to possess healing powers and protect the wearer against nightmares and evil."

"Well it's beautiful, and I love it," I said. "It matches the green on my hat, Grandpa! Look!"

I pulled the cap on and grinned as I hugged the soft blue afghan to my chest. "I love everything. Thank you."

Sun-burned and feeling happier than I had in weeks, I fell asleep on the couch by nine o'clock under Grandma's blue afghan, John Deere hat pulled over my eyes, and my peridot necklace resting in the hollow of my throat.

The rest of the week flew by and as we waved goodbye to my grandparents I realized I hadn't thought of Jessica once.

*＊＊

Mom looked surprised when I came downstairs after unpacking and taking a shower.

"You're still here," she said. "I thought you'd be gone to Jessica's the second you got out of the car."

I shrugged my shoulders and looked away. Truthfully, the closer we'd gotten to home and the more I'd thought about Jessica, the more my stomach had tied itself in knots. Part of me missed her, especially when we were laughing and having fun. But I realized I didn't miss the parts where we were stealing alcohol and breaking into people's houses when they weren't home. And I didn't like how she made me feel stupid when I felt guilty about doing those kinds of things.

"What's up, kiddo?" Mom asked, watching me carefully.

I glanced at her and shrugged.

"Nothing," I said and I headed for the fridge. "I'll call her later. She's probably doing stuff with her family this weekend too. I don't want to bug her."

Mom didn't say anything to that, but I could feel her watching me as I helped her make supper. I went up to bed right after, feigning a headache. I didn't call Jessica the next day either, although I lied and said I did. The day after that she was outside on the sidewalk when Mom sent me to the corner store.

I lurched to a stop when I saw her. She walked up to me, carrying her skateboard. She looked pissed.

"When did you get home?" she demanded.

"Um, a couple days ago," I said. "I was going to call you," I added quickly, lying. "But I haven't been feeling very good. Flu, Mom said."

Jessica stared at me, her eyes searching mine as I stood uncomfortably before her.

"You all better?" she asked, and I nodded.

"Yup. Going to the corner store for some stuff. You want to come?"

A smile bloomed across her features and I let out a breath of air. Then she did the most unexpected thing: she hugged me tight. I was shocked. When I'd left, she'd acted like she hadn't cared at all. I hugged her back. Maybe I'd been wrong.

"Welcome home," she said and she shoved a card at me. "Happy belated birthday."

I opened the card. It contained a packet of skateboard stickers. "Oh, cool!" I said happily. "Thanks, Jess!"

"Now tell me about your trip," she said.

I felt bad for waiting so long to call her, so I talked quickly as we walked. She complimented me on my necklace and she asked lots of questions about the horses.

"I love horses," Jessica said wistfully. "I've always wanted one."

"I didn't know that," I replied. "Have you ever ridden a horse?"

"A couple times, at summer camp."

"Cool."

We walked in silence for a bit, and then I remembered her dad had been coming home when we left.

"So how'd your week go? Did you have some fun with your dad?"

She shrugged. "He's pretty busy when he comes home. He's always fixing stuff around the house. Him and Mom had a fight on like, the second day. Something about Brian and school. I didn't see him much after that."

I opened my mouth to say something but she gave a happy little bounce and flapped her hands.

"Never mind that! Guess what?"

"Um, what?"

"I met a boy."

"Oh? Who? Some guy from school?"

"As if I'd ever date someone from here. His family has a cabin at Fox Lake. He's eighteen and he's pretty cool. I can't wait for you to meet him."

Eighteen seemed too old for Jessica, and I said so.

"It's only three years. I'm not a baby, Em. God," she said with a scornful laugh.

"What's his name?" I asked instead.

"Adam," she replied. "We're meeting at the park tonight. You have to come with me."

The knots that had been slowly loosening in my stomach clenched up again. Why would an eighteen-year-old, an adult, be interested in a fifteen-year-old girl like Jess? She was pretty—beautiful, even—but she was young. We were both young. It didn't feel right.

"Maybe…"

Surprisingly, Jessica didn't bug me about coming with her to meet Adam. After supper I figured out why. She let herself in around seven o'clock and crept up to my room. I jumped a mile when she opened the door and said, "Boo!"

Mom and Dad had gone to the neighbour's for coffee. I thought I'd locked the doors behind them. Jessica looked very different. She was wearing makeup, lots of it, and a tight yellow T-shirt that really showed off her boobs. She was wearing a denim skirt and white sandals and she had a purse slung over one shoulder. She looked much older than fifteen.

"Get ready!" she said urgently. "Adam will be at the park in half an hour."

"I don't want to go, Jess," I said.

"Please!" she begged. "He's bringing his friend Curtis, who is super nice. I want you to meet him."

"What? No way. This is a stupid idea. We're too young, they're probably already in college."

"God!" Jessica exploded and she stomped her foot for emphasis. "I knew you'd do this! You're such a friggin' *baby* about everything!"

"I am not!" I yelled back.

"Oh yeah? Then prove it. If you're really my friend, you'll come with me instead of letting me go alone. Now *that* would be a stupid idea."

I was furious. But she was right. Letting her go alone—and she would—was a bad idea.

I tossed my pillow at her and got off the bed.

"What am I going to wear?" I muttered, and she threw her arms around me, squishing the pillow between us.

It took a little bit longer to get me ready. Jessica had picked out an outfit which I firmly rebuked. We settled on a pair of white shorts and flowery off-the-shoulder top Jessica pulled out of the back of Mom's closet. She quickly did my hair and makeup while I called my parents and told them I was staying at Jessica's. By the time we headed to the park I was three parts nervous and one part excited. Maybe it wouldn't be so bad. Maybe they were nice, just like Jessica said they were.

Adam and Curtis were at the park when we walked up. They were leaning against the side of a dark-coloured four-door car. I thought they looked older than eighteen.

"Look!" Jessica whisper-squealed. "That's Adam on the right. Isn't he gorgeous?"

I said nothing, but I don't think Jessica noticed.

"Oh, and just so you know, they think we're seventeen. So play along."

My heart started to thump and my pace slowed. Jessica took no notice as she walked ahead, smiling and waving and calling out to Adam. The two guys looked at each other, then back at us, and grinned.

Adam was cute. He was about a foot taller than either of us and had short dark hair. He wore blue jeans and a grey T-shirt. His friend Curtis was a little taller and heavier. Not fat, just really solid. He reminded me of the farm kids who lived around Grandma and Grandpa's.

"Hey!" Adam greeted with a big smile, and he leaned down and kissed Jessica on the lips. "You look gorgeous. Who's your friend?"

Jessica grabbed my sweaty hand and dragged me forward.

"This is Emily. She's my bestie. Em, this is Adam and Curtis."

"Um, hi," I said quietly.

"Hey," Adam greeted.

"Hey," Curtis said. He gave me a thorough once-over that made my skin crawl.

"So, we're thinking we'd go for a cruise," Adam said as he walked Jessica around to the passenger door. "Maybe grab some food and a case of beer, then head out to the lake for a bonfire. Sound good?"

Jessica was already climbing into the seat.

"I guess you and me got demoted to the back seat," Curtis chuckled as he held the door open for me and stepped back.

"Yeah, I guess," I said.

I stared into the car. Jessica was laughing as she fastened her seatbelt. She looked back at me and gave me a "Well? What are you waiting for?" look. I stepped back.

"S-sorry," I said, backing away. "I just remembered something. I have to go."

Jessica scrambled to remove her seatbelt and leaped out of the car.

"Emily!" she shouted furiously as she stalked after me. "What are you doing? Get in the car!"

"No!" I shouted back. Tears began to run down my cheeks. "I'm not going. And you shouldn't, either!"

"Hey," Adam said, his hands spread wide in negation. "Nobody is forcing anybody here."

"Just *gimme* a second," Jessica snapped at Adam. Then she strode over to me.

"Goddammit, Emily!" she hissed, her fingernails digging into my arms. "What is wrong with you?"

I yanked myself out of her grasp.

"What's wrong with you?" I cried. "Jessica, don't go. Please! You barely know them."

She slapped me, one hard crack across the face. I staggered back, shock blocking out the sting of her hand on my flesh.

"Whoa!" I heard one of the guys say, then they laughed.

"Sorry," Jessica snapped. She stepped closer and opened her purse. "Look."

I just stared at her, my hand creeping up to my burning cheek.

"Look!" she insisted in an urgent whisper. "We'll be fine. If they try anything..."

I looked down. From the fading glow of the setting sun, I saw the glint of gunmetal and polished wood. She'd stolen Mr. Edwards' gun. She hadn't lost her stupid lip balm. I had been an idiot for ever believing in her.

I whirled and ran away.

Jessica called out for me twice, but I never looked back. I ran straight home, changed, scrubbed the makeup off my face and hung Mom's shirt back in her closet. I put on my pyjamas, crawled into bed and cried myself to sleep.

***

Mom wasn't surprised to see me come down the stairs in the morning.

"Hey," she greeted. "I saw your door closed last night and peeked in. You didn't stay at Jessica's?"

"No," I said glumly. "We had a fight."

"Sorry, hon," Mom said sympathetically. "Those things happen. I'm sure you'll make up in a day or so."

Nightshades

I said nothing but poured some juice and sat at the table as Mom read the paper.

The phone rang around nine-thirty and I shook my head when Mom raised her eyebrows.

"I don't want to talk to her yet," I grumbled. But I felt a surge of relief knowing she was okay.

Mom answered the phone anyway. She listened for a second, her expression hardening as she cut her eyes to mine.

"I'm sorry," Mom said, "but Jessica's not here. Emily said they had a fight last night and she came home by herself."

A pause as my heart thundered and my mouth went dry. My relief vanished as a cold lump of dread began to blossom in my gut.

"Yes, of course I'll talk to her. I'll call you as soon as I know more."

Mom hung up and sat down across from me.

"Jessica's not at home," she said. "She told her mom she was staying here and you told us you were staying there. You want to tell me what's really going on?"

A lump formed in the back of my throat and Mom's face blurred as I started to cry. It took a few tries but I finally managed to tell her about the two boys and the gun I'd seen in Jessica's purse.

"Oh my God," Mom breathed, her eyes wide and glistening. I don't think I'd ever seen her look so upset. "We have to call your father."

She did. He was on his way home to talk to me. I fought down a rising swell of panic. She picked up the phone—to call Jessica's mom back, I think—but I grabbed her hand.

"Wait," I said. "There's more."

And I told her all of it.

* * *

The police found Jessica Hasting's body two days later, out on Fox Lake. They never found the two boys...men...who'd called themselves Curtis and Adam. They never found Jessica's purse or Mr. Edward's old army gun either. One night I overheard Dad telling Mom that the Coroner had listed Jessica's death as an accidental drowning.

I never believed that. Not for one second.

I came back to Spartan once when I was in my twenties. I drove past the house where we'd lived for that very short, life-altering year, past Jessica's old house, the gas station where we'd stolen the cooler and the park where I'd seen her last. I passed the sign for Fox Lake on my way out of town, slowed, then changed my mind and sped by.

I glanced back in my rear-view mirror and my heart stuttered in my chest. A young girl in a yellow shirt, denim skirt, and white sandals stood at the entrance to the park. Her hands were on her hips, dark hair swirling around her shoulders. I swear I could see her dark eyes glimmering as she glared after me.

I slammed on the brakes, swerved to the shoulder of the road and scrambled out of my car. The sun was setting behind the trees and the scent of hot asphalt mingled with freshly cut grass. I stared back at the entrance to Fox Lake and felt goosebumps march up my arms as a cold sweat broke out down my back.

She was gone.

Lightning Source UK Ltd.
Milton Keynes UK
UKHW041830300421
382942UK00008B/385/J